HAN NOLAN

Born Blue

Harcourt, Inc.

SAN DIEGO   NEW YORK   LONDON

A portion of the proceeds from the sale of this book will benefit the
Monarch High School Project. The high school is committed to educating
and otherwise supporting homeless and at-risk teens in San Diego, California.

www.harcourt.com

Library of Congress Cataloging-in-Publication Data
Nolan, Han.
Born blue/by Han Nolan.
p. cm.
Summary: Janie was four years old when she nearly drowned due
to her mother's neglect. Through an unhappy foster home experience,
and years of feeling that she is unwanted, she keeps alive
her dream of someday being a famous singer.
[1. Abandoned children—Fiction.   2. Singers—Fiction.   3. Mothers and
daughters—Fiction.]   I. Title.
CURR   PZ7.N6783Bo   2001
[Fic]—dc21   00-12393
ISBN 0-15-201916-2

Text set in Janson
Designed by Cathy Riggs

C E G H F D

Printed in the United States of America

*This is a work of fiction. All the names, characters, organizations, and events
portrayed in this book are products of the author's imagination. Any resemblance
to any organization, event, or actual person, living or dead, is unintentional.*

For my sister, Caroline Walker Kahler,
thanks for the music

And for Brian, as always

Born Blue

chapter one

My first memory of myself I be drowning. I can close my eyes and feel myself getting pushed back under all that heavy water, my legs kicking and straining for the sandy bottom. Alls I find be more water rushing at me and over me, big walls of water hitting me whole and tossing me upside down, and I got no breath left, so I open my mouth and I swallow a gallon of salt water and choke, and more water get up my nose and burn in my head, and I go for a breath again, and the whole time I thinking, *Mama's gonna be mad at me, Mama's gonna be mad.* Then I ain't thinking nothin' and all the struggling stops, and I wake up in a dark room I know ain't mine. I think I be dead, but I scream, anyways, and a lady I never seen come in and holds me till daylight.

That were back when I were four years old. They couldn't find Mama Linda for a long time, and then when they did, they said I couldn't see her 'cause she were sick and needed help. I kept on crying for her and asking for her and telling all them grown-up people who now in my life that I wanted my mama. When were I gonna see my mama?

I got put in a foster home with Patsy and Pete, my foster parents, and some babies that come and went— there was always some babies in the home—and a foster brother named Harmon Finch.

I remember the house that Pete and Patsy lived in like I just moved out yesterday. I don't think after all these years I yet got the smell of that place outta me. It were in a town just outside of Mobile, Alabama, a little poky town. The house were a big old nasty with yellow paint and brown trim and mostly just fallin' down ugly. It had more puke smells in it than a toilet bowl, and all of them some kind of sour, like sour feet and sour cheese and wet sour and fart and BO. Most of them come from Pete, and the rest come from Pasty's cooking or the way she didn't never keep a house. Them smells just flooded the place, and weren't a spot you could go to get away from it but outside when the wind were blowing just right.

Only thing good about living in that home were knowing Harmon. It didn't take me any time to figure out that Patsy and Pete had no use for either of us 'cept to boss us round and make our lives miserable. All their attention went to the babies, so me and Harmon got to be best friends fast. Back then he a shy boy, seven years old and walking round with a shoe box everywhere. He carried it under his skinny black arm, and anybody got too close, anybody ask to see what he got in the box, he bring it round and hug it tight to his chest with both arms and twist side to side—sayin' *No!* with his body. Always when he said no 'bout something, he used his whole body. He were physical like that, and soon as we 'come friends he were huggin' me all the time, and I huggin' back, and never since have I felt safe and sure with a hug the way I done Harmon's.

Harmon were three years older than me, and when he little he were a skinny runty thing you wouldn't imagine could ever grow up to be much, but he grew up tall and round—not fat, just beefy. He got the friendliest face I ever seen in a person, too, with a big smile so full of goodwill it could melt anybody's heart, and it turns his own face so soft and good you fall in love with him right away; everybody do. He got happy round eyes, and eyelashes so long he got to cut them to look a man, and chubby cheeks that make him look too young and sweet for any kind of hell raisin', but he say that be fine by him.

In the foster home those babies come and went so fast, weren't worth it to bother looking at them and learning their faces, but me and Harmon stayed on and stayed so close you knew if you saw one of us coming you saw the other. Patsy and Pete, thinking they was being cute, called us chocolate and vanilla 'cause of our skin, and it just burned me up to hear it. I didn't like being called vanilla or anything to do with white. White was Mama Linda and her not coming to see me, and Patsy and Pete and their steely meanness, and the evil-eye lady with the pistol in her boot who lived across the street and talked all the time 'bout shooting us and hanging us out for scarecrows in her cornfield. No, I didn't like white.

Harmon showed me what he got in the shoe box—cassette tapes of lady singers. He got Aretha Franklin and Ella Fitzgerald and Odetta, Sarah Vaughan, Etta James, Billie Holiday, and Roberta Flack. I couldn't read all that till I were six years old, but there were a Fisher-Price tape player in the house, and one time I said to Harmon, "Harmon, what's on them tapes? Can I hear?"

"Be music," he said. "They my daddy's tapes."

We dug out the tape player from a pile of toys we was supposed to keep in a box in the basement. We listened in front of the toy box 'cause we knew if a toy wandered too far from that box, we got the strap.

We listened to the ladies singin'. I laid down on the floor on top of a rug that smelled wet and sour, and Harmon laid down next to me, and we stared up at the ceiling that looked like white cardboard and listened to those pretty voices. Sometimes while I were listening I'd look at the pictures of the ladies on the front of the cassettes, and I'd look at the words I couldn't read, and I'd get all happy and easy feelin' inside. I loved the ladies. I loved their singin'.

Pete and Patsy wanted to know what we was doin' down in the basement so quiet, and they said we doin' dirty things, and I felt all twisted nasty hearing their ugly words.

It were our secret 'bout loving the ladies. We'd go outside and climb into the Japanese maple tree Patsy said were the only tree we allowed to climb, and talk our secret talk 'bout loving the ladies.

"They pretty, Harmon," I said once.

"Mm-hmm." Harmon nodded.

"They make me happy."

"Me, too," Harmon said. "They make me want to jump."

"You want to jump out the tree?"

"I want to jump and jump and turn myself around."

I said, "They make me want to sing. Harmon, I want to sing." I said that and I felt something inside me go different from everything else I ever felt. It felt like something strong were sitting inside me. Like it were sitting in my belly waiting on something, and it made me feel hungry. I got to feeling so hungry I thought there weren't enough food in the world could fill me up.

"Harmon, let's go see if they got any bread to eat," I said.

After that time, when I thought of the ladies, when I heard the ladies sing, I had to eat bread so I didn't go feeling that hunger. I'd eat the crust first and then roll up the rest into a ball, dip it in the sugar bowl, and suck on it, getting all the sweet out of it, and then I'd eat it down and start on another one.

Patsy wanted to know why I ate so much bread. She

said I looked like dough. Said maybe she should pop me in the oven and see if I bake. I stayed clear of her best I could.

Sometimes we would go sit in the Japanese maple tree with a stack of bread and eat and dream the ladies' music till it would get so late we 'bout fall right out the tree asleep.

That whole time I lived with Patsy and Pete and Harmon and the babies that come and go, I loved Harmon and the ladies most, and almost every day I lived there, which lasted almost three years, we'd go to the basement and listen to the ladies sing. But Harmon didn't dance and I didn't sing. We was too scared to get the strap. We'd lay on the sour rug and dream we was singin' and dancin', and I had me a stack of bread on a plate by my side for when I got so hungry I thought I would die.

chapter two

WE HAD A SOCIAL WORKER who come visit us every once in a while to see how we doing, and ask what we thinking. Her name be Doris Mellon, and she were a fat lady who always wore happy red dresses and red lipstick and red fingernails and had the blackest, shiniest skin I ever seen. I used to love to pet her arm and grab her skin and hold it. When I got to know her better I used to kiss her arms and her cheeks, and I were jealous 'cause I knew she loved Harmon best. I knew 'cause she come over one time and said to Patsy that she gonna take Harmon out to her church on Sunday and that she wanted to do it regular. She wanted to take him out with her every Sunday.

I never been to no church. Weren't sure, even, what church were, 'cept Harmon were gonna get to go with Doris and I weren't. Doris said that she would take me someplace special, too, sometime, but I wanted to go with her and Harmon. Why couldn't I go? I wanted to know. So did Harmon. He asked, "Why cain't she go? She my best friend. Don't wanna go no place without my Janie." And Doris and Patsy looked at each other and shrugged their shoulders, and I got to go.

The church were a long drive away to a building that looked like a movie theater. There was lots of people, and they was every one of them, 'cept me and one lady, black skinned. I smiled big when I saw this, and everybody smiled big right back at me. The preacher did his shoutin' and prayin', and the people sitting in the chairs shouted *amen* and *hallelujah* and waved their arms about and stood up and sat down and sang. A whole roomful of people was singin'. I grabbed ahold of Doris's skin and Harmon's shoulder, and I hung on tight. A whole roomful of people singin', and I got chills inside and out. I wanted to fill myself up with bread, but there wasn't none, so I sucked on my lower lip. I wanted to sing so bad, but I didn't know the sounds or the words. I just knew about Aretha and Odetta and Ella. I knew their sounds, but the people in the church was singin' new ones.

After church Doris took us out to Shoney's for lunch and chocolate ice-cream sundaes. We never had sundaes before, but I got hooked on them first bite I took. I knew weren't nothin' in the world ever taste as sweet and good as a chocolate ice-cream sundae, and I always let some of the syrup dry on my lip so I could lick on it later.

Harmon and I couldn't wait to go to church with Doris every week, and I didn't know what I loved most about it—being out with Doris and Harmon, the music in the church, or eating sundaes—I were just happy as happy could be the whole time.

After three weeks of going to the church, I had learned most the words and all the tunes to them songs they sang regular every week, and I tried singin'. I were going on almost five years old, and I hadn't never sang a note. I opened my mouth to sing but didn't hear nothin'. I could feel sound humming in my chest, but I couldn't hear it. I opened my mouth more, like the men and women standing up front with the blue-and-gold robes on, and I sang louder, and I could hear my own self singin'. I were making a song, my first song. I shook my shoulders and clapped my hands like the people all round me, and I sang louder. I felt Doris let go of my shoulder, and I heard her stop singin'. I turned my head, and Harmon were staring at me and smiling. I looked up at Doris, and she smiled, too, so I knew it were okay me singin', so I kept on.

Every time we had to sit down and listen to the talking, I got antsy and hungry and I couldn't wait till the singin' started up again.

After church that day, Doris said to me, "Child, you sounded real pretty singin'. Didn't she, Harmon?"

"Yes, ma'am, she do. And she can sing other. She can sing Aretha song and Etta and Roberta."

We was riding back to the stink house in Doris's car, and me and Harmon was sitting together in the back. I gave him a kick on his leg.

"Hey, you messin' up my one good pair of pants. Now quit."

I said, "How you know what I can sing, Mr. Harmon? You don't know what I can do."

Doris looked at me in her rearview mirror and said, "Sing something for us, Janie. Go on, it's all right. We're all friends."

I looked at Harmon and he nodded. "Go on, thang, you can do it."

Didn't never hear myself sing alone before. I closed my eyes and felt myself down in the basement, laying on the sour rug, listening to Roberta Flack. I heard her voice singin' "The First Time Ever I Saw Your Face," and I started singin'. And sitting in that car with my eyes closed, singin', felt like entering those pearly gates of heaven I were always hearing 'bout in church, felt like chocolate ice cream with chocolate syrup, nuts, whipped cream, and a cherry slippin' down my throat. Felt like the first home I ever known.

chapter three

MAMA LINDA COME to see me. I were coming home from kindergarten, riding on the bus with Harmon. She were waiting at the end of the road where the bus driver always let us off, standing with one leg crossed in front of the other and her arms folded 'cross her chest. She were butter blond and blue eyed and pretty as pink pastries, and kids on the bus was sayin' it had to be my mama 'cause I looked just like her.

I got down off the bus behind Harmon and peeked round him at Mama Linda. She smiled big and opened her arms out. I went on and ran to her, feelin' funny 'bout it 'cause I weren't sure yet if I felt happy to see her or what. She hugged me, so I hugged her back, and my arms closed round her skinny, skinny waist. She smelled like I remembered, even though I forgot I remembered. She smelled like a cake made out of sugar and flowers and cooking oil.

"Now, how's your little face today?" she said, like we just left off seein' each other yesterday.

I didn't know what to say, so I looked back at Harmon, who were behind us.

He had his hands dug in his pockets, and when I looked at him, he shrugged and his face drooped so sad like he was giving up on me, saying good-bye 'cause Mama Linda be there, comin' to take me home.

I reached back for him and grabbed his arm, which were still pushin' at the bottom of his pocket, and said, "This here Harmon. He be my brother now."

Harmon said "hey" to Mama Linda, with his head down so low his fat cheeks was 'bout all I could see of his face. Then he pulled away from me and ran ahead to the stink house without us.

"He's a shy one," Mama Linda said.

"He don't know you," I said. "Are you here pickin' me up? Am I goin' home with you?"

I didn't know what I were hoping the answer would be till she told me no. Then I knew I were hoping she coming for me, 'cause soon as she said no, I wanted to push her down on the road and run off home with Harmon.

Mama Linda stopped walking and pulled my two arms toward her and stooped down in front of me. "Janie, I've been...ill. I've been in a rehabilitation center 'cause I've...I've had this amnesia thing." Mama Linda nodded to herself and said "amnesia" again.

"What that be?" I asked.

Mama Linda set her head at a tilt and took a bit of my hair in her hand. "Don't you talk funny now. Amnesia's when you lose all your memory. You can't remember anything. So, see, I didn't even remember I had a little girl. That's how ill I was."

"Are you all better? Why cain't I come home?"

Mama Linda stood up. "Well, see, they've got to watch me awhile, still, and make sure I don't go back on—get that old amnesia thing again. You wouldn't want me to get it and leave you alone at the beach again, would you? So, for now I'll just come visit you, and if things go well"—Mama Linda started up walking again—"then we'll live back together."

ONCE A MONTH MAMA LINDA come to visit, bringing a sack of boiled peanuts in her hands and handing them off to me like that were the reason for coming. I always ate them up before she left, popping in one after another and swallowing them whole like they was vitamin pills. I got sick every night on days when she visited, and Pete said it be the peanuts, so he said not to eat them no more, but still I got sick. I didn't tell no one but Harmon.

"Harmon, I sick again."

"What you gonna do?"

"I gonna go get me some food 'cause I think it a hunger sick in my stomach."

I waited for Patsy and Pete to go on to bed, then I

slipped down to the kitchen in the dark and stashed down as much food as my body could hold. Next day, Patsy did have a fit and then some when she come down and found all her food gone missing. She blamed me and Harmon both, 'cause she said no way could I eat all that food myself, and she told Doris on us.

I said to Doris, "It ain't Harmon, but Harmon get the strap same as me, an' you gotta tell Patsy it ain't Harmon."

So Doris and Patsy talked long, and they got up a plan so I don't be gettin' in trouble and gettin' sick. Doris give me Mama Linda's phone number and said once a week I could call her and talk, and on days when Mama Linda come, Patsy would set out extra food for me to come down and eat at night if ever I felt sick-hungry.

First time she set the food out, she wagged her angry finger at me and said, "But if you eat anything else besides what I set out, you'll be standing on one foot all day for punishment and so will Harmon." She knew she could get me to do right if she punished Harmon for what I done wrong.

"And thanks a lot for telling Doris about getting the strap, as if we're here beatin' you senseless. One time standing on one foot and you'll be begging for the strap."

When Mama Linda come, I always asked if she be better now, and every time she said yes, she was gettin' better every day. She never said nothin' again 'bout me coming to live with her, though, and when I called her every week like I supposed to, Mama weren't never home 'cept once. That time I got her, she said I just caught her on her way out and she'd call me back tomorrow 'cause she gotta run, but she didn't never call me.

Me and Harmon talked 'bout me one day leaving and going back to live with Mama Linda, and he said he didn't want me to never leave 'cause we belonged always together. I knew he were right 'bout that, 'cause I loved Harmon and the ladies most in the world, but I knew if Mama Linda ever said, "Come on," I'd come on, 'cause I knew it were just the way it had to be, and I felt sad inside for never telling Harmon this.

Mama Linda kept coming most every month, and one time she brung a boyfriend with her. They took me out to a playground. The boyfriend looked too bored, so the next time, she brung a different boyfriend, and we just stayed outside the stink house and did nothin'.

I never liked any of the dudes she showed me, but just in case, I always asked if they—any of them—be my real father. That's when Mama Linda got creative, makin' up stories, one time saying my father be famous so she had to keep him a secret, and the next time saying she don't even know who my father be, 'cause she had a case of amnesia back then, too.

Sometimes Mama Linda would forget to come see me, and lots of times she didn't stay long and took me nowhere, and lots of times she got real angry at me 'cause now she were s'posed to come out to see me twice a month and it were messin' up her other plans.

"Grown-ups like to do grown-up things," she said. "I got plans, little face, so I got to cut this visit short. When you grow up, you'll understand what I mean, but you call me, okay? You can always call me. Here, now, I brought you some candy to share with Herman."

I always knew when the visit were gonna be short, 'cause she'd wear something black and sexy that showed off her boobs. On days when she stayed long, she wore baggy jeans and kept her boobs tucked in. I liked her best on her long-visit days, even when we didn't get along.

She were always trying to pick fights with me. One fight she tried to start, she said I acted too much like Harmon, only she called him Herman. "You two are always whispering. I don't like it. It's rude. What are you two saying, anyway? Are you whispering about me? You like making fun of me?"

"We ain't talkin' 'bout you, Mama Linda. We just talkin'."

"I don't like that boy. He's too quiet. It makes me nervous. He's always studying me and grinning. What's he grinning at?"

"Don't he have the sweetest smile you ever did see?"

Mama Linda hated me not fighting with her, but I knew if I did, she wouldn't never come back, so I never said thing-one against her. Then one time Doris said Mama could take me for a weekend visit, and Mama took me to a motel. Soon as we pulled into the parking lot I got scared, 'cause there be a outdoor pool right at the motel, and last time I were out with Mama Linda, I almost drowned and she disappeared.

"Why ain't we goin' home?" I asked. "I thought we goin' home."

"We're supposed to stay in town, little face. Maybe if this visit goes well, I can take you for a home visit sometime, but that Doris said we've got to stay close by for now. But that doesn't matter, does it? I'm never home much, anyway."

"I know," I said.

Mama Linda pointed across the parking lot. "Look, they got a swimming pool over there, and I bet there's a Coke machine right around the corner from our room. We can drink cola all night, if we want."

"I ain't goin' in no water," I said.

"Sure you are, little face. You can swim in your underwear if you don't have a suit. You'll be precious. Everyone will think you're just precious."

Mama Linda had a look on her face like she was seeing it all right in front of her, everyone thinking I be precious and her getting all the glory for it.

I didn't have to worry long 'bout drownin' in no pool, though, 'cause Mama didn't stick around long enough hardly to do much but pee. Soon as we stepped into the room, she put down the overnight case she brung along with her and run off to the bathroom. I stood in the doorway, waiting.

"Doris said you can sing," she said after she got off the toilet and come back into the room, zippin' up her jeans. She looked at me. "Well, come on in the room and sing. Let's see what kind of good singer I've got me."

I didn't move or say nothin'. Mama Linda put her hands on her hips and said, "Sing!" And her voice were angry, just like that.

"I cain't sing," I said.

"Doris said you got a pretty voice. Now, come on. Come on, little face, sing."

I turned round facing out the door and said again, "I cain't sing."

Then, before I knew it, Mama Linda were shovin' me out the door and scootin' me back out to the car, and we screeched out the lot and back onto the highway.

"You won't sing, I'm taking you back to Patsy. That's the way it's going to be, okay? You going to sing?"

I shook my head with my chin sitting on my chest. Much as I wanted Mama Linda to take me back with her, I couldn't do it. I couldn't sing for her.

Mama Linda sped on to Patsy and Pete's, saying she didn't care what I told on her to Doris, she were sick of that fat-ass woman sticking her nose into her business, anyway.

She didn't take me all the way to the house. She pulled up to mine and Harmon's bus stop and told me to get out. "I'll come see you when you're ready to sing, so if you ever want to see me again..."

She didn't say more. I climbed out the car, and she drove on, slow, like she were thinking I gonna come running after her.

I caught her looking in her rearview mirror at me, and I turned from her and walked on toward the stink house. Soon as I did, Mama Linda pulled away with one long screech of burnin' rubber. I just kept walkin' on. I just kept walkin'—and singin'—'cause only thing I knew to do to keep that sick-hungry feelin' away were to sing.

chapter four

FOR MORE 'N a year Mama Linda been comin' to see me, but she told Patsy she weren't never comin' back so now Doris could give me away for adoption. Doris told me not to worry. I just had to let Mama Linda cool off awhile.

Me and Harmon said we was happy being just us two again, but I was sad for wanting Mama Linda back sometimes, and Patsy said I was turnin' into a fatso feedin' myself up the way I did when I got to thinkin' 'bout it. Sometimes, when no one were in the living room, I tried callin' Mama Linda on the phone. Two times I got her, and both times she hung up on me.

Then Mr. James and Mrs. James come to visit us. They both had soft brown skin matching exactly like they was brother and sister, and they was both tall and skinny, too, but Mr. James had big teeth and spoke all quiet and smooth. Mrs. James spoke smooth, but she weren't so quiet and she laughed a lot. I thought they come to see me, 'cause no one never come to see Harmon before, but they come for him. They told him he could call them Mama and Daddy if he wanted to, or John and Cherise. Then they took him off somewhere for a couple of hours, and when they brung him back Harmon were changed. He wouldn't say nothin' to me hardly at all. He wouldn't say what be going on, and I got scared and raided the refrigerator that night even though Mama Linda hadn't come in months and wouldn't stay on the phone when I got hold of her. The next day after school, Patsy made me stand wobblin' on one foot till supper time for punishment for eatin' all her tomatoes. My ankles burned so much, even if I did cheat and change legs when she weren't looking.

One Friday afternoon I couldn't find Harmon on the bus and I cried, and kids called me a baby 'cause I were almost seven and I were cryin', but I didn't care, 'cause all I cared 'bout was knowing where Harmon gone.

Pete were sitting on the front stoop drinking a beer when I got home. He saw my face and said, "What you been bawlin' about?"

"Where Harmon at?" I asked. "He not on the bus with me."

Pete waved me away. "Aw, he's gone off for the weekend with that James couple. They're gonna adopt him. They're gonna be his parents now."

"I ain't never gonna see him again?" I could feel hysterics shakin' my shoulders.

"Calm down, girl. You'll see him Sunday. He ain't gone yet."

I hid out in the basement all weekend, sucking on balled-up bread and feeling scared 'cause Harmon took his tapes with him like he wasn't never coming back. At night I got sick-hungry, but I knew I couldn't eat up the kitchen no more, so I snuck outside to the lady's house across the street—the lady with the pistol in her boot—and I didn't care what happened to me. I climbed her peach tree and ate on her unripe peaches till I felt sick. Then I went on back to the stink house and yakked it all up in the toilet.

Harmon come back to the house on Sunday and he had a book of photographs under his skinny black arm and he said it were his life book and it told the story of Mr. James and Mrs. James and their house and their dog and the school where Harmon were gonna go and everything else Harmon could think he might wanna know. He showed me his book, and then he showed Patsy and Pete, and then he looked through it on his own with me watchin' him, and Harmon were so full of happy he didn't see how I were dyin' all over. He told me that him and his new mama and daddy went fishin', and he showed me a picture again of the fishin' hole. He said they took him to a football game, too, and how he met a boy his same age, named Max, who lived close by, and how he were gonna have his own room and his very own toys that didn't have to go in a box, and how Mr. James took Harmon to his office and let him play on a computer and Mr. James said Harmon be a fast learner. Harmon couldn't stop talkin' to see how every word he said were just killin' me.

I asked him to come on and listen to the ladies with me, and we got down on the rug same as always, only it weren't the same 'cause while Aretha were singin' Harmon kept on talking right over her voice like her voice didn't hold nothin' for him no more.

I stopped the tape 'cause I couldn't bear what he were doing, and I said, "Ain't we never gonna see each other now, Harmon?"

Harmon sat up and shrugged, and he hung his head down low over his lap. "Don't know." He looked up. "But you always be my best friend, Janie."

TWO WEEKS LATER Mr. James and Mrs. James picked up Harmon for good. They had their dog in the car, droolin' on the window like it couldn't wait for Harmon to be his. But I couldn't let go. I hugged on Harmon and cried an awful mess, and Patsy kept trying to pull me off, but I just got right back on him. And Harmon were crying, too, and he whispered that he loved me most, even more than the ladies, and all of me were so tore up it felt like I was bleedin' to death.

Pete got me off Harmon and hustled him into the car while Patsy held tight to me so I couldn't latch on to

Harmon no more. The car started rolling away, and I got screaming, the hurt were so bad. Then the car stopped, and I thought they was gonna give Harmon back to me. I hushed up and I saw the back window roll down.

Harmon called to me, and I ran to the car, wantin' to reach in and snatch him through the window.

"Here, this yours now," he said. He handed me his tape of Etta James, my favorite, and I took it and sat down in the drive with the tape in my hands and cried hysterics over losing Harmon and the ladies till my voice run dry.

chapter five

I WERE SINGIN' my own kind of blues after Harmon
and the ladies gone away. I climbed into the Japanese
maple tree and sung my made-up songs, holding my
sound long and bending the tune with my hurt. I sang
any words that come to my head, 'cause it didn't matter
the song, it just mattered the singin'. All I wanted to do
anymore was go down to where my songs would take
me, down deep to that place that cut and healed, and cut.

Didn't hear nothing from Harmon for a long time.
Then I got a package in the mail with his name on the
return address. Inside I found a shoe box different from
Harmon's raggedy box. This one were new. I opened it
and it smelled of new shoes, only weren't shoes in the
box. Were tapes. Harmon's note said he and his new dad
recorded the ladies for me so we could both have them.
Asked would I send back Etta James so he could make a
copy of her, too. At the end he wrote, "Love, Harmon
W. James." He and Etta had the same last name. I told

Patsy, who stood behind me with a baby in her arms, looking down at what I got.

"Harmon got the same last name as Etta James now," I said.

Patsy said, "James is a common name. Don't go making something big out of it, Janie. You always got to make something big out of everything."

"You think they know Etta James?"

Patsy shifted the baby onto her other hip and said, "Now, what did I just say? No, they don't know her. Woman's probably dead, anyway. I don't know why you two are always listening to those dead people. Now, here"—she handed me the baby—"he's put a dirty in his diaper. Go change it and don't forget to wash your hands. Oh yeah, and Doris won't be taking you to church this Sunday."

I had started out the kitchen door but I turned round. The baby were pulling on my hair, pulling it cross my face, so I couldn't see Patsy good.

"Why ain't she taking me?"

Patsy turned away and picked up another baby from the high chair.

"I got a call saying her daughter died."

"She got a daughter? She got a daughter who dead?"

"Yeah. What did you think? You think she don't have a life outside of you?"

I pulled my hair out of the baby's hands. He were stinking bad but I kept standing there.

"How old her daughter be?"

Patsy shrugged and set her baby in the sink. "She's grown up. She's probably my age."

"How old you be?"

"I'm thirty-six, miss nosy britches. Now go on and change that baby's diaper before his butt stains." Patsy yanked her baby's shirt up over its head and took the dish-rinsing hose and sprayed it at the baby.

"What her name be?" I asked.

"Who? You mean Doris's daughter? It's Leshaya. Was Leshaya. Why? Don't you believe me? You think I made it all up to make your life miserable? Think I got nothing better to do than make up ways to keep Doris away from you?"

I turned and walked away with the baby, thinking on the name Leshaya. Were a pretty name, Leshaya—a real pretty name.

chapter six

LESHAYA. I SAID the name to myself all afternoon. I
took it to bed with me and slept with it close on my
tongue so when I woke up the next day it were the first
word I spoke. I loved the sound of it—gentle, easy
sounding, just as easy as a breath. Saying it and hearing
the sound of it made me feel quiet inside, peaceful, like
sitting in a empty church with Harmon and Doris before
it filled up with people.

I carried the name with me to school that day, keeping it in my head and not saying it loud for others to
hear, 'cause I weren't ready to share it yet. Just like with
the ladies and their singing, I needed to keep the name
to myself and think on it awhile. During math I spelled it
out different ways on a piece of paper over and over, and
I covered the page with it—Leshaya, Lashaya, Lisheya.
It spelled out just as pretty as it sounded, no matter how
I spelled it, but I picked Leshaya. I thought how I

wanted that name for me, for keeps. I wanted everybody to call me Leshaya.

Riding on the school bus that afternoon, I were thinking that when I got to the stink house I would say to Patsy and Pete, "My name be Leshaya," then see what they do, but Mama Linda were hiding in a bush near my stop and jumped out at me before I got walking far on the road to the house. Her hand shot out from the bush and clamped down on my arm and yanked me so hard she 'bout snatched me outta my shoes. She said, "Come on," and I did 'cause I had no choice. I went on with Mama Linda to a white car waitin' on the road on the other side of the bushes. She said for me to scoot on in the back, and I did. She climbed in behind me, and before I could remove my backpack, turn round and get sitting with a seat belt and all, we was outta there. I got myself strapped in and looked up to the front. A skinny-faced white lady with babylike teeth were looking back at me, smiling, and a black man with a couple of mean scars on his face were driving the car.

"Janie, this is Mitch and Shelly," Mama Linda said.

The lady up front stuck her hand out and said, "I'm Shell."

She had a wild, jazzed-up look in her eyes, almost like she were gonna eat me soon as she could.

The lady shifted a look at Mama Linda, waitin', I think, for Mama Linda to explain or say something else to me.

"We're taking you away from that stink hole you've been living in," Mama Linda said. "You're glad about that, aren't you?"

"Yes'm, I reckon," I said, and Mama Linda nodded at Shell and said, "See, what'd I tell you, polite and sweet and pretty."

I smiled inside myself 'cause I knew she were talking 'bout me. Shell nodded, then said to me, "Hey, you hungry? We got you a chicken sandwich at the Chik-fil-A."

She turned round and fished 'bout for the sandwich, and Mama Linda said for Mitch to take a left and the signs would take us out to the highway. I saw Mama Linda's hands trembling, and her eyes looked 'bout as wild as Shell's. She had on makeup, but it didn't cover up her yellow-lookin' skin, and she had on her usual strong flower oils she wore for perfume, but it didn't hide her stink—a strange kind of rotten smell.

"Where we goin'?" I asked.

"You're going to Birmingham. Won't that be nice?" Mama Linda said. She didn't look at me. She wiped her mouth. Her lips were sore chapped.

I shrugged. Didn't know nothin' 'bout Birmingham 'cept it were in Alabama somewhere.

"You want your sandwich with or without mayo?" Shell asked me.

"Don't matter," I said. "Am I never gonna go back to Patsy and Pete?"

Shell handed me a sandwich and looked fretful at Mama Linda like I said something wrong.

Mama Linda said to me, "You won't ever have to go back to that terrible place again. Shell and Mitch are going to take care of you now."

"Shell and Mitch? Do Doris know 'bout me goin'?"

"No. Now listen, Janie. This has got to be a secret, okay? Now, Mitch and Shell are good people and they love children"—Shell nodded—"and they're gonna be really good to you. All you got to do is be their daughter. See, you got to call them Mama and Daddy. Think you can do that?"

I looked at Mitch. He were keeping his eyes on the road, but I could see some of his face and I could see his arms and his hands on the wheel, and what I thought was that even if he weren't black as black like Doris, he were black right on, so I nodded.

Mama Linda slapped my leg and said to Shell, "See, what'd I tell you."

Shell reached back over her seat and touched my hands. "I love you already. I'll take good care of you, sweetheart."

I pulled my hands away from her, making like I needed to unwrap my sandwich, 'cause I didn't trust no jazzed-up white lady tellin' me five seconds after knowing me that she loved me. I looked at Mama Linda. "What 'bout you? Where you goin'? Why you ain't my mama?"

"Of course I'm your mama, little face. I'm your mama Linda and she's your mama Shell, but it's Shell who's going to care for you. Look how she bought you that sandwich. I didn't even think to get you something to eat. So she'll be your mama. Now that's the deal."

I wondered 'bout her saying the word *deal*. Doris used to say that word when she took me and Harmon out for Sunday lunch. She said we was always playin' *Let's Make a Deal*, 'cause of the way we was always trading our food with each other. I asked Doris what a deal be, and she said it were like agreeing to do something, and me and Harmon was agreeing to make a trade with our food.

So I asked Mama Linda in that car, "You make a deal with Mama Shell?"

Mama Linda got squirmy, moving her legs like they ached and looking away from me out the window. "Well—yeah. Yeah, okay, we made a deal."

"A trade? You make a trade?"

Mama Linda leaned forward and tapped Mitch's shoulder. "You can let me out here. Here's fine. I can walk the rest of the way."

"We're almost to the exit," Mitch said. "Let me get you off the highway."

"No, it's okay. I need to walk. I need to walk, Mitch!"

Mama Linda's voice got hysterical, just like that. One minute she were saying pull over, and the next she were screaming how she needed to walk and she opened the door like she gonna jump out the car.

Mitch swerved off the road, and Mama Linda got out and walked away up the ramp of the exit.

We didn't say nothing for a long time. Mitch pulled

out on the highway again, and we rode on. I sat with my chicken sandwich unwrapped in my lap, and Shell turned to face front.

Then after we been silent a real long time, Shell turned round and said, "We've got to change your name. I have a sister named June. We'll call you June."

I said, "My name gonna be Leshaya."

Shell and Mitch snatched a look at each other, and Mitch asked, "Who's Leshaya?"

"Me," I said. "I be Leshaya now."

chapter seven

I KNEW I BEEN kidnapped but didn't care none. What's it matter who done the snatchin'? Them at Social Services yanked me from Mama Linda and gave me away to Patsy and Pete, then Mama Linda stole me back and did a deal with Daddy Mitch and Mama Shell. Ain't no difference, really. None of it had thing-one to do with my feelings. So what if I been kidnapped? I figured Mama Linda didn't just hand me over to any old body. She did a deal with my daddy; musta been my real daddy, 'cause why would she give me away to strangers?

Mama Shell tried to call me June and Juney, but I wouldn't come 'less she called me Leshaya, so she learned right quick I were a stubborn, pigheaded child, just like Patsy always said. But she didn't take the strap to me or make me stand on one leg, neither. She called me Leshaya.

First night in their home she caught me crying 'cause I were scared and missing Harmon and the ladies and

Doris, and she said she couldn't do nothin' 'bout Harmon and Doris but we could go to the music store and I could pick out some brand-new music for myself.

We went shopping the next day. I didn't find all the same tapes as them Harmon had, but I found some I never heard sung by the ladies, and I got a extra one by Etta James. Mama Shell got me a new tape player, too, the kind that fit on the waist of my pants and had earphones so I could listen private without nobody else hearing. I could lay in my own bed at night and listen all I wanted till I fell to sleep, and weren't nobody tellin' me no, and no babies laying in cribs next to me screaming for daylight.

Sometimes, when I were singing my songs, laying on my bed, I wondered if anybody were ever looking for me. Did Doris remember me? Did Harmon wonder whatever become of me? Were Patsy and Pete happy I were gone from them? I'd fall asleep wondering these questions, and in the morning Mama Shell would say to me at breakfast or while she were doin' up my hair, "You walked in your sleep again last night."

"Did I? Where I go?"

"Same as last time. You walked over to the phone with your face grinning and your eyes bright and as wide open as can be, and you mashed the numbers like you were making a call." Mama Shell squinted her eyes and studied me when she said that.

"Who I be callin'?" I asked.

Mama Shell said, "I thought *you* could tell *me*."

I shrugged. "Don't know nobody's number."

Mama Shell said I could hurt myself walkin' in my sleep, but I knew she didn't like me trying to make a call, 'cause maybe I would call someone who could get her in trouble. That's why I didn't say how I knew Mama Linda's number. I didn't tell her how I were maybe callin' Mama Linda in my sleep. Anytime Mama Shell saw a cop, even if he be in a car goin' the other direction, she 'bout had a fit. She'd tell me to duck down or act natural or stare the other way. Never knew what she'd want me to do, so I always froze till she said move. Seemed Mama Shell were awful nervous 'bout getting caught with me. She were always looking to see if anyone trailing us, always checking her rearview mirror.

Mama Shell got thinkin' that I gonna try to run away or tell on her for stealing me, but I said, "Why I gonna do that? You treat me better than Patsy and Pete anyday."

It were true, too. And our house didn't stink, neither. The inside smelled like a stack of clean clothes just passed through the house, 'cause Mama Shell did a lot of laundry. Didn't know where it all come from, but she were always doin' a load and cleaning up something. She told me I needed to wear deodorant so I wouldn't smell like a onion, and she washed my hair every day and sometimes gave me a bath twice a day, so I went around wearing my skin too tight all the time.

She loved doin' up my hair, and some days I'd go to school wearing one hairdo, and soon as I come home, she'd do me up another. She liked to say how her hair be real blond like mine and how Mama Linda's hair be dyed and weren't real. She said it like it be bad that Mama Linda had dyed hair and good that she had her own color on her head. She liked pointing out what made Mama Linda look bad and what made herself look good. Once she said she knew 'bout me drowning in the Gulf of Mexico. Said she saw it in the newspapers.

I told Mama Shell 'bout the amnesia that made Mama Linda forget she even had a child; I told her that's why I almost drowned, but Mama Shell said, "Now, I don't want you to tell anybody what I'm about to tell you, especially your daddy Mitch. He doesn't want me telling you this, but you've got a right to know. It wasn't amnesia. Your mama wasn't sick with amnesia. She's a drug addict. She takes drugs—heroin. She's a heroin addict. It's nasty stuff. It'll do you a bad turn."

I looked at Mama Shell and her eyes looked like firecrackers going off, just full of sparks. And I come to recognize that look after a while. It were her I'm-telling-something-dangerous look.

I said, "My mama take drugs?"

"Yes, but don't say I told you so, okay?"

"Where she get drugs?"

"Huh?" Mama Shell's eyes went dry—dead.

"Where she get them drugs?"

Mama Shell grabbed my shoulders and turned me round so she could get at my hair again. "How am I supposed to know where she gets it? Probably from the streets, like everybody else. Now, hold still. That Linda's dirty. She must be living on the streets, she's so dirty. Aren't you glad you live in a nice, clean house? Doesn't your mama Shell keep a clean house?"

Mama Shell did work hard at keeping things clean, rubbin' and scrubbin' the way she did. It were like the world were one big stain she just never could rub clean. I made friends okay at school, 'cause I were pretty to look at and had pretty hairdos and clean clothes, so I could thank Mama Shell for all that.

First day at school I heard Mama Shell explaining to the principal how her and Mitch and me was new in town. She gave the principal phony records, phony birth certificate, phony everything, and nobody said thing-one 'bout it. I didn't mind, 'cause all my new records said my name be Leshaya and said I had good grades in math. Never did do well in math before.

I told the kids in my new class that I had a mama who were white but I had a African American daddy, so I were part black-skinned even if it didn't show. I held up my arm and let them look close, and I said how just under all that white were the black layers and if you looked closer you could see it. Most said they couldn't see nothin' but white, but my new best friend, Shanna, said she could see it all right, and so could I, so it didn't matter zip what anybody else said.

I were proud of my daddy Mitch, and I thought next time I saw Mama Linda I'd ask her if he be my real daddy, just to make certain sure I were right 'bout what I thought, cause 'cept for the scars, he were good lookin'. He had a wide face with flat high cheekbones that Mama Shell said were because he be part American Indian. He wore his black hair straight down his back and parted in the middle, and he had a wide nose with big round holes for nostrils, and a good juicy-lookin' mouth, and deep narrow eyes that looked full of smarts, like everything he knew 'bout life he learned by watchin' and he stored it all right there in his eyes.

The thing I figured 'bout Daddy Mitch were that he loved gold and money best in the world. He had a gold tooth right in the front of his mouth, and he wore a gold watch, and chains round his wrists and neck, and gold stud earrings, and gold buckles on both sides of his leather jacket he were always wearing. He carried a fat wad of bills on him, and he loved taking it out and counting it, especially whenever Mama Shell were fussin' at him for doing something she didn't like. Only problem, Daddy Mitch didn't want nothin' to do with me or Mama Shell. I found this out first time I tried talking to him. I wanted to know 'bout his scars. I wondered what kind of accident made them pits in his cheek? I asked him and he said, "Shut up."

Anytime I tried talkin' to him, that's what he said. He wouldn't never talk to me, but he didn't talk much, anyway. Weren't never in the house for long. Most nights we didn't know where he be at. Mama Shell said he went to Miami on business lots, and that's why he weren't never home. One time she said she thought he had another wife down there in Florida, but then she laughed when she noticed she spoke out loud and I were standing in front of her hearing what she said. "I'm only fooling, Leshaya, so wipe that worried look off your pretty face." And she laughed some more, but her eyes was shootin' off them dangerous firecrackers.

chapter eight

MAMA SHELL LOVED to shop. She loved to pick me up after school and take me to the mall. Seemed her purse were full of dollar bills, but she didn't always pay for what we got. She could move through a store so natural that even when I seen her taking something, I weren't sure of her stealing, till we got home and she dumped out the loot. She used to work in a department store that had a handheld gadget that could remove the big plastic tags off clothes. She took it with her when she quit and kept it in her purse to use on any clothes we liked so we wouldn't set off alarms, walking out the store. I felt proud the way she could haul off stuff and not get caught. She could have a real innocent look about her when she wanted. Most of the time, though, Mama Shell just looked classy. She wore her hair big and stiff with hair spray, and she wore makeup that made her whole face look pink as pink. When we went to the mall, she always wore a skirt that fit snug around her skinny body, and her feet always hurt 'cause, she said, her shoes weren't sensible.

We shopped at the toy store last. Mama Shell paid for my toys with real money, and I felt proud of her for that, too. My favorite toy be my first doll, a doll with black skin and pretty black hair in tight curls and happy brown eyes. I named her Doris, 'cause she 'bout black as Doris, and I sang her my songs. I sang the old songs, the ones I couldn't find at the music store. I sang them so I could remember them.

Every day I missed Harmon and Doris. I missed listening to the ladies and suckin' on my bread in the basement with Harmon. Mama Shell had me on a diet 'cause, she said, my breasts shouldn't oughtta be growin' when I'm just seven years old. And they was growin', but I were scared I'd get to looking too skinny like her. Seemed white women always trying to get skinny, always trying to lose what make them women in the first place. Patsy, Mama Linda, and Mama Shell didn't none of them have any tits or ass to speak of. And I didn't care if I grew up big like Doris, 'cause I knew if I were big, I'd be nice and folks would want to hug me and lean on me and fall asleep on me 'cause I'd be so comfortable and sweet-smelling in my powder and perfume.

One night I were laying in my bed, singing my songs from memory to my Doris doll, and I had my eyes closed and the headphones on my head even though I didn't have no tape playing. I couldn't hear nothin', so I 'bout fell out the bed when Daddy Mitch got hold of my arm and shook it. It were dark enough in the room that I couldn't read his face, but his voice sounded strong like maybe he was angry. He asked me, "Is that you singin'?"

I didn't know what to say, 'cause who else could be singin'? But he asked like he wanted a answer so I said, "Were me singin', Daddy Mitch. I didn't know you come home." I sat up in my bed and held Doris close to me. "Don't you like music? Do I be keepin' you 'wake?"

He said, "Child, you got a voice on you."

"Yes, sir," I said. "Doris say I sing pretty."

"I never heard a child sing like that before." Daddy Mitch shook his head. "You got a voice like butter. It's rich. Rich and smooth as smooth. *Mm-mm*." He shook his head again and walked out the room.

THE NEXT DAY, Daddy Mitch told Mama Shell he would take me to school, and Mama Shell got those sparks flashin' in her eyes, so I knew she didn't like him driving me and she were thinking something dangerous. But she let him take me, 'cause even though he weren't home much he still the boss of our house.

I had to tell him how to get to the school. He weren't hardly paying attention though, 'cause he wanted to know 'bout my singin'.

"Who taught you to sing like that?" he wanted to know.

I said, "The ladies taught me: Etta James and Sarah Vaughan and Aretha Franklin. I got their tapes, and other tapes, too. I been listenin' to the ladies since I were real little. Me and Harmon." I looked at Daddy Mitch. "You know Harmon?"

Daddy Mitch shook his head and I pointed to the sign for the school. "Harmon my best friend. He my foster brother. We used to all the time listen to the tapes, and Harmon say he gonna dance to them and I say I gonna sing. You know what? Singin's 'bout the best thing I know to do. Even if I sad, singin' feel real good to do. Know what I'm sayin', Daddy Mitch?"

Daddy Mitch pulled into the school lot and I showed him where he could park. He said he didn't need to park, he'd just let me off, but I told him I wanted him to walk with me to my class. He made a face that showed off his gold tooth and said, "Why the hell do I have to do that?"

I said, "Don't have to. I just want you to. I want to show everybody you my daddy."

Daddy Mitch looked at me like he was wondering, *What in the world?* I pulled at his arm and he said, "Damn," and shook his head. But his eyes looked happy and he come on with me to the class.

After that day, anytime Daddy Mitch come home from somewhere, he called me to come give him a hug and sing him a song. He dug a old guitar out from under his bed. He said he had that guitar since he were fifteen years old. Said he once loved it so much, he used to sleep with it at the foot of his bed before Mama Shell come along. He laughed at that, but Mama Shell didn't. She gave him her dangerous look. She didn't never seem happy to see him no more, and when he were around she didn't look happy to see me, neither.

Daddy Mitch weren't too good at playin' the guitar, which surprised me 'cause I figured him being my real daddy, he'd be musical. I knew how bad he were, 'cause I listened close to the guitars the ladies got playing in the background of their songs. I knew the sounds of all the different instruments playin' in the background even if I didn't know all their names. Weren't nothing I hadn't heard in them songs. I knew them so well, I figured if I had the chance all I had to do were to pick up a instrument and I could play just what I been hearing all my life. But I liked Daddy Mitch playin' the guitar, 'cause that way I weren't nervous 'bout singin'. And seemed my singin' made him happy, so I didn't mind doing it. I got real used to it, even, and Daddy Mitch come around a lot more to the house.

Only problem, Mama Shell didn't like it. Said my voice were too big for a little girl like me. She said it sounded like a grown-up were singin' behind me and I were just moving my mouth. Said I be flirtin' with Daddy Mitch and that a seven-year-old singing saucy songs 'bout love were dirty.

I got to worrying 'bout Daddy Mitch coming home, 'cause of the way Mama Shell acted with the two of us. Worrying got me wishing Mama Shell allowed bread in the house, 'cause my stomach were always grumblin' for it. Singin' were all I had left to keep the worry away, and I just prayed Mama Shell wouldn't take that from me, too.

Daddy Mitch said Mama Shell's nerves was coming unraveled. Said she were getting paranoid about everything and troubling trouble when there weren't no cause. Daddy Mitch said for Mama Shell to take these pills he dug out of the sports bag he were always carrying round with him. He gave her tiny red pills—tiny red pills that made her stupid.

chapter nine

EVEN WITH DADDY MITCH talkin' to me nice and singin' with me, times was always better when he were gone and Mama Shell and me could be on our own, just shoppin' and paintin' our toenails. Mama Shell would act forgetful and sleep past the time to pick me up at school sometimes, and I'd have to ride home in a taxi and wake her up so she could pay the driver. But I were happier when it were just us. Times was just always calmer with Daddy Mitch gone.

I turned eight, then nine, and my memories of Harmon and Doris and Patsy and Pete faded, but my Mama Linda memories stayed sharp. I knew she were round somewhere, 'cause once in a while I got a whiff of those flower oils she liked to wear. I could smell them on Daddy Mitch's clothes sometimes when he come to pick me up at school. I could smell it in his car like she were just sittin' where I were sittin', not more 'n five minutes earlier.

I asked Daddy Mitch once if he been with Mama Linda, 'cause I could smell her in the car, and he acted like he gonna choke.

"Why you asking me a thing like that?" he said, coughing, his deep-set eyes tearing up and his nostrils sucking in. "Ain't seen your mama in years."

I knew it weren't true, but Daddy Mitch had a temper, so I didn't say nothin' more 'bout it. Every once in a while, though, those oils was all over him and I knew she been comin' round, maybe asking 'bout me, maybe wanting to see me. But she couldn't see me no more 'cause she made a deal, and Daddy Mitch and Mama Shell were gonna raise me.

I tried calling Mama Linda from the mall once when Mama Shell was off tryin' on too many clothes and said I could go get me a ice-cream cone to eat. I called her just to tell her how I be okay and how I know she been comin' round and maybe worryin' 'bout me, but like usual, she weren't home. I let the phone ring sixteen times and she never did pick up.

Mama Shell noticed the flower oils smell on Daddy Mitch, too, and once she said right in front of me, "You've been going round with Linda. I can smell her on you. She's been touching you."

Daddy Mitch said, "Them pills is makin' you stupid." He looked at me. "Don't talk in front of Leshaya. Leshaya, you run on and get your bath like you was plannin' to do."

I left the room and hid out in the closet just round

the corner. They didn't notice no bathwater were running in the pipes, 'cause they was fightin'.

"Baby, you know Linda's got to pick up her junk," I heard Daddy Mitch say. "Of course you smell her on me. What's got into you, anyway? You gettin' stupider and stupider."

"Linda doesn't need to be touching you for that. You reek. You reek of Linda. You don't think Leshaya knows? You don't think I know? You're the one who's stupid if you think we don't notice."

Daddy Mitch smacked Mama Shell and tore out the house. I heard him speed off in his car, and we didn't see him for a good long while after that.

Mama Shell took more pills. She took pink pills to help her sleep, white ones to make her not so stupid from the red pills she were still taking to keep her happy. I didn't think none of them worked too well.

I turned ten and February come, and as usual in my school in February, the music teacher had us singin' civil rights songs and Negro spirituals and gospel songs. Most times in music I did like everybody else and I either sung kinda quiet and like I were bored, or I shouted. I knew if I sung out in my real voice I'd get too much attention, so I never sung much. But for some reason that year I were tired of the same old songs and the same old stupid kids singin' their same old stupid way, so I didn't sing at all and Mrs. Ringold noticed. Tuesday after Tuesday she noticed me not singin', and finally she said if I weren't gonna participate I could march myself right on down to the principal's office. I didn't know why, but I weren't feeling too good that day. My stomach were grippin' me tight, kinda pulling down between my hip bones, making me cranky. When Mrs. Ringold got after me this time I didn't stay quiet like usual. I said, "Ain't nobody singin' it right, anyway."

"What's that?" Mrs. Ringold asked.

I sat up in my seat, feeling even crankier, the pain in my side real sharp. "Ain't nobody in this whole school know how to sing these songs. Everybody sing like they babies."

"Well, Miss Leshaya, maybe you can teach the class how to sing. Why don't you come on up front and sing this song the way you think it's supposed to be sung."

Mrs. Ringold had on a face like she thought she got me good, so I sashayed on up to the front, ignoring my side pain, and turned myself round to face the class. Then I belted out "My Lord, What a Mornin'" loud enough for the whole school to hear me.

When I got done singin', nobody did nothin'. It stayed quiet for a whole minute at least, and I felt proud of myself, but sick, too. It felt like my insides wanted to drop right out between my legs.

Then the class clapped for me and they did that for a while and then Mrs. Ringold held her hands up for them to stop.

When Mrs. Ringold finally spoke, her voice sounded puffed up and breathless, and she said, "Why, Miss

Leshaya, I have never in my life heard such a beautiful, strong, voice, coming from such—"

"Scuse me," I said. I hated to miss out on my chance for glory, but I knew something were about to happen that I needed to find a toilet for, so I ran out the room and down the hall to the bathroom. I didn't know if I should sit down on the toilet or stand over it, 'cause I didn't know where the sick was gonna come out. Finally I sat down and I found bloodstains in my underpants.

I were ten years old when I got my first period. I had tits bigger than Mama Shell's and I were almost as tall as her, too. I got to thinkin' with my grown-up voice and my grown-up looks that maybe Mama Linda got my age mixed up and I were really fifteen and not ten. But Mama Shell said, no, that were just the way girls do. "Some grow faster than others," she said, looking me over, her face pinched up with disappointment.

I changed after that day in music class with Mrs. Ringold. I got sassy and loud and spoke my mind, and I didn't hide my voice. Mama Shell said when girls get their periods they get cranky and unreasonable every now and then 'cause of hormones shifting in their bodies. Seemed like I were always cranky, though.

Everybody in school had heard what I done that day. Mrs. Ringold came by the school early the next morning and pulled me out of my regular class to talk to me 'bout it.

She sat me down in the principal's office and she sat

across from me at his desk. I looked round the room, wondering where the principal had got to.

"How come you never sang like that before?" she asked me.

I leaned forward so my arms could rest on the desk. I felt like I was her age, 'cause sittin' down we was the same height and 'cause I had my period and Mama Shell said that made me a woman.

I said to her, "I were just trying to fit in, but I be tired of that. You got to teach them kids how to sing, not just teach the songs. We singin' our songs like we just screamin' or bored. Every song be different. Every song got its own feelin', but nobody know but two feelings in this school: screamin' and bored. You got to get us better songs, too. We tired of your old songs. We been singin' them same songs for three years now."

Mrs. Ringold didn't look like she appreciated my advice, but didn't matter. I were already sittin' in the principal's office and weren't nothin' else she could do.

She asked me where I learned to sing. She wanted to know who my voice teacher be. I said, "Etta James be my voice teacher."

"Well, I'd like to meet Miss James. She's done a wonderful job."

"Yes, ma'am, she has, but you cain't meet her 'cause she dead or famous or something. I learned her off my tapes."

I dug into my backpack, which were sittin' at my feet. I pulled out my Etta James tape and handed it to her. I didn't listen to the tape much anymore, just carried it round for company. I could hear her voice and her songs in my head without the tapes. Still, when Mrs. Ringold asked if she could take it home and listen to it, I couldn't let her do it. I popped up outta my seat and grabbed the tape back. "You can buy your own at the music store," I said. I was just as sassy as could be, and Mrs. Ringold didn't do nothin' 'bout it.

I felt powerful from what I said to her. I felt powerful standin' over her with my Etta James tape held up in my hand, away from her. I stared at her hungry-looking face and I thought, *Cain't nobody kidnap me, or take from me what I love most in the world ever again if I be powerful like this all the time.* And that's how it happened. I seen what I got to do to get what I want. See, in a instant I grown up. In a instant I took hold of my own life.

chapter ten

OVER THE NEXT two years, I got famous in my town for my singin'. I sung solos at every chorus concert and Mrs. Ringold always saved me for last on the programs. She said she liked to build anticipation. People in the audience cheered when I stepped down off the bleachers to sing my songs, and they even stood sometimes when I sang. They was always show tunes and not what I liked to sing, but Mrs. Ringold said parents come to hear show tunes. I sang anyway 'cause I loved the attention it brung me. I loved hearing the audience clapping, and seeing them standing up for me. A couple of different times I sang at some teachers' weddings, and I were real popular at them, too. All the teachers was proud of me. It were like the whole school were famous and special 'cause of my singin'.

The only person who didn't like all the attention I got were Mama Shell. She got upset with me 'cause my picture were in the papers all the time. Once a news station come to the school and did a story 'bout me, braggin' how I be just eleven years old and singin' like I were Aretha Franklin. Mama Shell were sure someone would find out she stole me. She didn't like how they said my age on the TV, and that they asked me questions and taped a bit of me singin'.

I told Mama Shell to stop worrying, 'cause I didn't even look like my old self no more. Since turning eleven I wore my hair in tiny braids all over my head. Mama Shell would take the braids out every couple of weeks and do them over and it felt like she were running tiny iron rods into my skull every time she took apart a braid. It just hurt to move my hair round after it were twisted for so long, but I loved the braids, and even though Mama Shell were always wanting to do me other hairstyles, I wouldn't let her. I just liked the bitty braids.

When I turned twelve I went to the middle school, and weren't just my hair I wore different; I made Mama Shell get me different clothes, too. I wanted to show off how I got tits and how I got a nice round ass like the other black girls in my school. I weren't like Mama Linda, all skinny and flat-chested, and I were proud of how I looked. But Mama Shell said I looked just like Mama Linda, dressin' the way I did, which just goes to show how stupid them pills of hers was making her.

I wore shoes that made me taller than most all my teachers and taller than Mama Shell, and she didn't like that one bit, neither. I wore eyeliner and eye shadow and mascara and lip gloss, and my lips was full and shiny, and glossin' them up always made me feel I were black. Dressing and looking the way I did, I felt my whole body were black. Were the first time in my life I felt right in my body.

Mama Shell wouldn't stop fussin' at me 'bout the way I were lookin' and behavin'. She sat me down at the kitchen table one rainy afternoon and said, glaring at me hard, "We got to do something, Leshaya." Her brows were drawn together like she were fierce angry, but she looked so shrunken and pale without her pink makeup and no eyebrow pencil to darken up them blond brows of hers, so I didn't think her anger carried much weight to it.

"What you mean?" I said. "Do something 'bout what?"

"I want my little girl back," she said, still looking hard at me. "I didn't bargain for this. You weren't supposed to look like this for a long time yet." She pointed at my chest.

I shrugged and sat back in my chair. "Cain't help how I change, Mama Shell."

"If you were my *real* daughter you wouldn't look like this."

I lifted my chin. "How would I look, then?"

"My little girl—my little girl..."

Tears ran down her face. They just squirted out in a instant and ran down her face. Her face got red, too, and it didn't look healthy. I wondered if she needed one of her nervous pills.

"Where you got your pills, Mama Shell? Let me get you a pill."

Mama Shell's hand shot out and smacked my face good. "I don't need those damn pills! You keep away from me with those pills!"

I jumped up from my chair, my hand on my hot cheek, and Mama Shell dove for me, catching my other hand and pulling me toward her.

Her voice whined. "I want to tell you about my girl, my little girl. I had a little girl once."

"What you mean? You mean beside me?" I sat myself back into my chair but sat back far enough that she couldn't grab at me.

Mama Shell nodded. "She had dark hair and eyes like Mitch, but she had freckles on her nose and little Kewpie-doll lips like me, and she was the sweetest, happiest child there ever was." Mama Shell closed her eyes and pinched herself at the bridge of her nose, like that would hold back her tears. She shook her head. "She was so precious. She loved playing Barbies." She opened her eyes and, looking cross, said, "You never loved doing that! All you ever loved was that Doris doll. You never loved me. You never once said you loved me!"

I crossed my arms in front of my chest and said nothing.

Were true what she said. Never did say I loved her, 'cause 'cept for the ladies and Harmon, I didn't have lovin' feelings for nobody. I tried not to think about it much, but sometimes, when I did, I found weren't nothin' inside me no more. Seemed the only true feelings I had left were angry feelings.

I watched Mama Shell stand up from the table, holding on to it, case she fall. "Where's the damn tissue?" she asked. She stepped away from the table with her bony arms reaching out for the counter like she blind, and I saw her hands shook as they was movin' over the countertops and opening cabinets. The lady was strung out bad. She found her some tissue in the bread box and came wobbling back to the table, with the tissues shakin' in her hands.

"What color were your little girl, then?" I asked.

I weren't sure this child were for real, but I asked, anyway, to keep her mind off me not loving her and 'cause I wanted to know.

Mama Shell honked her nose into the tissues and sat back down.

"She was like café au lait," she said, her eyes fillin' back up with tears. "She had beautiful skin, real soft skin. She didn't have any hair on her arms."

My body got all tense with her telling me this. I leaned forward toward Mama Shell, forgetting I were trying to stay out of reach. "Where she be now?" I asked.

"She's dead." Mama Shell pinched at the bridge of her nose again. "She had a heart attack. My baby had a heart attack."

"A heart attack? How old were she then?"

"Seven. She was just seven years old. You're not supposed to die of a heart attack at seven years old, are you?" Mama Shell looked at me, waiting like she wanted a answer from me.

I didn't have one. I sat back again and let go my breath. Didn't know why, but I were glad she died. Guess I didn't want to see no café au lait daughter of Daddy Mitch.

Mama Shell put her head down on her arms, so she were talking to the floor, and said, "I want my little girl back. I just want my little girl."

I didn't know if she were talking 'bout me or her own child, but I didn't think it mattered to her. She just wanted a little girl, any little girl, but I couldn't be little no more. I knew too much.

chapter eleven

I HAD ME SOME new friends in middle school but they wasn't close like Harmon been. Never could keep a friend longer than a couple of weeks, anyway. Anytime I got me a new friend, I'd feel all singsongy inside thinking this time it gonna last and we gonna be best friends forever. But we always ended up fighting soon enough, and it weren't never my fault, neither. Weren't my fault their toys and stuff were made cheap and broke easy, and I just give Lizzy a little push and she falls and breaks her wrist like I pushed her hard, when I didn't. It were always something like that, where I got the blame for it all. Didn't matter, anyway, 'cause didn't need no friends; I had my Etta and Odetta and Aretha.

The new friends in the middle school be different. They like little puppies trottin' after me, wantin' to be round me 'cause I looked grown and 'cause I got this voice and 'cause I just as sassy-assed as they come. They thought I were acting cool. Weren't just the girls yappin' at me, neither. Boys was wanting to be round me and touch me all the time, especially the seventh graders. They was always telling me how pretty I be, that I got pretty eyes and pretty hair, but they wasn't looking at my face or head when they sayin' it—they looking at my tits.

I felt funny with them looking at me, so I smacked their faces when they got their eyes where they didn't belong. They come on after me, anyway. Acting sassy like that, and singin' the way I could sing, got me more friends and attention than I ever got before.

Then Mama Shell got it into her mind that she wanted to move. She told Daddy Mitch she be desperate to move.

"We've got to get out of here," she said, crawling up to Daddy Mitch, who were sitting on the couch. "I don't know what I'll do if we don't move. We've got to go soon, Mitch. Things are getting too hot around here. You said so yourself. Come on, Mitch, let's go." She whined and tugged at his shirtsleeve. "Let's get out of here."

Daddy Mitch pushed her off him and said, "Shell, I can't just leave. I got business here, good business."

"But you said the cops were sniffing around. They're sniffing around! We've got to move, Mitch."

Any time Daddy Mitch come home, Mama Shell would get on him 'bout movin', so Daddy Mitch didn't come home. Mama Shell said one day that we was just gonna have to move without him, but we never did. I agreed with Mama Shell, though. I didn't see no cops sniffin' round, but I seen how dangerous Mama Shell been acting at the mall. She weren't careful 'bout stealing stuff no more, and a couple of times some salespeople caught her, but she managed to sweet-talk her way out of it. I got nervous going into the stores with her. I were sure some mall guard were gonna haul her off to jail one day.

I tried finding excuses not to shop with her, like sayin' I wanted to go look at books or something I knew she didn't like. She'd let me go off, and I'd just wander round tryin' on lipstick and perfume samples and callin' up Mama Linda on the pay phones and never getting nothin' but lots of ringing and ringing. But one time at the mall I heard singin'. There were a whole group of people singin' gospel music, and I told Mama Shell I had to go listen. "You go on and shop," I said, "and I'll meet you at the food court."

I didn't wait for her to agree with what I said, 'cause I were just drawn to the singin'. I run off down the mall, following that music.

I found the group in front of the food-court fountain. They was standing spread out in rows up on a couple of stands, and they was singin' and swayin', and all the people was black and dressed up nice—the men and boys in suits and the women and girls in dresses.

There was chairs set up in front of them, and didn't look like I had to pay nothin', so I sat down to listen to the music.

They had some good singers up there, real good. Hearing them singin', and seeing the small audience holding up their arms and swayin' and sayin' *amen* made me want to go up on that stage and sing, too. I wanted to show them how good I sung. The feeling were so strong in me it made my throat hurt, like a song got twisted and stuck halfway up my windpipe. I never got to sing no real gospel at my school, and Mama Shell and Daddy Mitch didn't go to no church. I bad wanted to get up there and sing. Hearing them singin' felt like I was back with Doris and Harmon, sittin' in church. If I closed my eyes I could pretend I were with them again. And maybe it were 'cause I been thinking 'bout Doris and Harmon that I noticed one dude, standin' the third row back, who had eyes just like Harmon's. They was big and round with way-long eyelashes, and they had that same too-sweet look in them the way Harmon's did. He were a big old thing, though, tall and heavyset in his body, with wide shoulders. He'd grown out of his suit, too. I saw that when he come forward and played the trumpet. His shirt cuffs showed too much, and his shoulders looked like they gonna bust through the top of the sleeves any second. He didn't look comfortable. His face were all sweaty, too, but his playin' sounded good. I couldn't keep my eyes off him, and I noticed he kept snatching looks at me. The second time he played the trumpet, when he got done and were about to go back to his place in the rows, the music leader held out his hand like he introducing the trumpet player and said, "Ladies and gentlemen, Harmon James."

I jumped up out of my chair, forgetting where I were, and shouted out, "Harmon!" Other people stood up, too, and clapped, but I pointed at him and shouted his name again. "Harmon!" I weren't thinkin' right. In the middle of their show, I pushed out of my row of chairs and ran onto the platform and grabbed my Harmon. I guess people thought I be crazy, 'cause they pulled me off him, but I shouted, "It's me, Harmon. It's Leshaya."

Harmon backed away. He was lookin' at me hard but shakin' his head no, like he didn't know me. Then I remembered. He didn't know Leshaya.

"I mean, it's Janie," I said. "Harmon, it's Janie from the stink house! Remember? Patsy and Pete? Harmon, it's me." The whole time I were saying this, the gospel singers was holding me back, away from my Harmon. I could feel tears on my face, and I kept sayin', "Harmon, it's Janie. It's Janie."

It seemed like forever before he finally said "Janie?" like he understood. Then, at last, at last, we was huggin' each other and crying with each other, and Harmon wanted to know where I been, but the music leader said Harmon had a show to finish. Me and Harmon said we sorry, and I got down off the platform. The people in the chairs clapped, and I noticed a big crowd had filled in so that all the chairs was taken and more people was stand-ing in bunches behind them.

I didn't want to sing no more after that. I just wanted to talk to Harmon, and they was words caught in my throat instead of song. I thought the singin' never would end, but it did, and me and Harmon got back with each other. I were crying and hugging him, and he were doing it, too, to me, and in between all that, I told him where I been and what happened, and he told me how good his life be with his mama and daddy and how he got a baby brother now.

Strangest thing besides seeing him all big and chunky were his talkin'. He didn't talk like me no more; he talked smooth like his parents. He talked like he readin' out of a book. He told me he sung with his church and played the trumpet in a high school band, and hearing him, my aching in my throat come back and I were long-ing for a wad of bread.

"Listen to you, Harmon. You sound all—all different. You so happy and smilin'. Ain't never seen nobody as smilin' as you before."

"I'm doing really well," he said, nodding his head too much. He kept on nodding while looking me over, and he said, "You look so different. You look older than I do now. I can't believe it, Janie."

"It Leshaya now. I named myself after Doris's girl who died. You know her girl died?"

Harmon bowed his head like he prayin'. "Sure," he

said. He looked back up at me, and his eyes shone happy and sweet even though he sounded sorry. "Doris moved a couple of months after her daughter died. Moved way out to Wisconsin. I had a different caseworker the rest of that year, and then I didn't need one anymore because Mama and Daddy adopted me."

We kept talkin' long as we could, and we traded addresses and phone numbers, and I warned him how we might be movin' 'cause Mama Shell always talkin' 'bout it. I told him 'bout my singin' and how music were still the best thing in the world to me. "Still ain't nothin' better than singin' my heart out," I said, and Harmon nodded too much again, like he were thinking so many thoughts, he forgot he were doin' it.

I told him about Mama Shell and Daddy Mitch and about school, but I left out everything about how sassy-assed I acted, 'cause I could tell Harmon were real fine and wouldn't approve of the way I been acting. That left me with a sadness 'cause we always been close, and not telling about all of myself put a space between us that weren't there before. Couldn't help it, though. I wanted him to be proud of me, so I stood straight with my feet together and my hands behind my back, and 'cause his voice were soft and quiet, I made mine that way, too.

Then the music leader come by and said we had five minutes before they had to start for the buses in the parking lot. I grabbed Harmon, and he hugged me and said, "I love you, Leshaya. I love you even more than the ladies."

I cried all over his shrunken suit, and he said good-bye and I said good-bye and I told him how I loved him, too, even more than the ladies. But when I watched him walk away from me, I knew I were lying. I still loved Harmon, but I loved the ladies most.

chapter twelve

I DIDN'T SEE MAMA SHELL sneakin' up on me. I were still waving at Harmon's back when she come along and near sent me up through the skylight she scared me so. "Who's that you're waving at?" she said. "He some-one from school? Are you meeting boys at the mall? Is that why you've been slipping off every time we go shopping?"

"No, ma'am. No, it ain't. I promise."

Mama Shell smacked my head. "You don't promise. You're lying. I saw you with him. I saw you practically climbing all over him in front of everyone. Now, come on."

Mama Shell dragged on my arm through the mall and through the parking lot, and even though I could have fought her off and run, I didn't, but I didn't say nothin' 'bout finding Harmon, neither. She were so paranoid already, I knew she would think Harmon gonna go tell the police 'bout her stealing me. She didn't say nothin' while we was driving home, but when we got inside the house she smacked me 'bout the head awhile and told me I better keep away from those bad boys and I better make sure they keep their hands to themselves. I let her hit on me a bit, 'cause it didn't hurt and she needed something to do to get out her anger. Then she told me to get out of her sight, so I run off to my room. I grabbed up my Doris doll and my headphones and turned on my tape of Etta James and let her singin' cut through the layers of me. I let her music cut down to my soul. I took a deep breath and let it out, and everything felt all right again.

After a while of listening to Etta and then Billie Holiday and Odetta, I felt safe enough inside to think 'bout my meeting with Harmon. He were so different but the same, too, when I thought 'bout it. He grown up big, but so did I. His voice were all polished off, like he a teacher. That made me feel funny, like we didn't come from the same place no more. He were the one taught me to speak, and then he went on and changed his voice on me. And his voice were so soft and kinda high-pitched. I couldn't imagine a voice like his ever yelling at nothin'. I could see how good and fine a boy he'd grown to be, too, and bein' with him, I felt like who I been weren't good enough.

The ladies never done that to me. They never changed on me. They just sang. I knew they gave me the most important thing in my life. They gave me their voices and their songs. Weren't nothin' better in the world than that. If I could sing all the time, if I could be like the ladies and sing for my living, sing for all my life, well, wouldn't matter if I didn't turn out so good as Harmon. Nothin' else in the world would matter if I could sing and people would listen. Ain't nothin' else in the world like singin'.

chapter thirteen

I ALWAYS FIGURED I would live with Mama Shell and
Daddy Mitch till I were all grown up, but when I been
still just twelve years old, my time with them come to a
end, and I didn't never see them again.

I guess the beginning of that story happened when
Daddy Mitch moved his business into our house. He and
Mama Shell carried boxes and bags of stuff down to the
basement one afternoon, and when I asked what be goin'
on, Mama Shell looked up at me with her firecracker
eyes and said Daddy Mitch were moving home and we
was gonna see a lot more of him from now on.

Daddy Mitch said, "Don't you come snoopin' round
down here, though. Hear what I'm sayin'?"

"Yeah, Daddy Mitch, I hear, but what's all that you
carrying down them steps?"

"None of your business. You keep out, and things will
be real happy round here."

"Yes, sir," I said.

I don't know 'bout happy, but they was busy. People was always stopping by to see Daddy Mitch. They wasn't always the best-looking people, neither. Some fancy dudes dressed in suits would come and strut on through the house like they owned it, but much more come all ragged out, like they bums off the street. If Daddy Mitch be out when they come, then they all shaky and nervous, pacing round back of the house and checkin' the road to see if Daddy Mitch be comin'.

Daddy Mitch told me a long time ago he were a salesman, and when I asked what he sell, he said, "Life." He cackled at that, like he said something funny, but that kind of laugh scared me, so I stayed off the subject. I were little when I asked, but now I were twelve, almost thirteen, and I had a pretty good idea what he were sellin'. But it weren't till one day when school let out early 'cause of a cafeteria fire, and I took a taxi home, that I found out for sure. I got home when I weren't supposed to, paying the taxi driver with my emergency money Mama Shell been givin' me for when she don't come pick me up, and who did I see beggin' and clawin' at Daddy Mitch out in our yard but Mama Linda.

I ducked to the side of the house and listened to Mama Linda whining to Daddy Mitch, saying she should be able to pick up stuff whenever she wanted.

Daddy Mitch laughed and said, "Baby, it don't work that way. It's bad enough I got to give out your junk for free. I ain't givin' out extra just 'cause you run out early. I've told you that before."

"Free!" Mama Linda screeched. "You got Janie. I gave you my Janie. I didn't get nothing for free. I got to live the rest of my life without my Janie."

"Don't you try that on me," Daddy Mitch said. "I ain't buyin' it. You traded her off for heroin. You sold your own child for heroin."

Mama Linda were crying and I could hear them moving off away toward the back of the house. I slid along the other side, trying to keep hearing what they sayin'.

I missed something, 'cause when I got to hearin' them again, Daddy Mitch were yelling at Mama Linda. He said, "You want her? Take her! Go on and take her back. We don't need her. Go on! I'm tired of you. You take your girl, and get on outta here."

Then Mama Linda said that she didn't mean what she said and that he weren't so tired of her last month, and her voice changed to being all sweet and sexy, no more yelling, but Daddy Mitch didn't take none of it.

He said, "I ain't givin' you nothin'. You don't come around here no more. You want Leshaya, take her. You don't, that's your problem. The shop's closed! You get your junk somewhere else from now on."

Daddy Mitch slammed inside the house, and Mama Linda pounded on the door some and when she finally gave up, she said, "You'll be sorry. You're going to be so sorry."

I hadn't seen my mama in over five years, and I only reached her once in all the times I tried callin' her from the mall, and even then, she were too stoned to make much sense. So when I knew she were leavin', I come from round the house and looked at her good. She walked toward me, lookin' straight at me, but she didn't know who I be. She weren't too steady on her feet, didn't seem to me, and she were way skinny so her veins showed on her forehead real sharp, and her eyes looked way big and her head looked big, too. She had her hair tucked up under a baseball cap, and just a couple of greasy strands hung down on the side of her face.

When she were just 'bout to pass me by, I said, "Mama?"

Mama stopped, looked me up and down, and said, "Janie?"

I nodded and Mama Linda looked at me again. Her eyes was more bloodshot than eyes. Didn't know how she could see out of them. "You look just like me when I was your age," she said. "How old are you? Sixteen? Seventeen?"

"Twelve."

"Oh." She looked round herself to see who might be listening, then she said, "Listen, I want you to do me a favor. You know where Mitch keeps his stuff? You know how to get at his stuff?"

Mama Linda were talking fast and low and grippin' my arms too tight. I could feel electric current running through her to me. I could feel it in my arms and it hurt.

"You got to get me some…"

I raised my arms, with her hands still hanging on them, and flung them down hard, breaking myself free of her.

Didn't say nothin'. I just walked away.

chapter fourteen

I HAD A LOT to think on that day, but weren't nothin' 'bout Mama Linda. I weren't gonna let what she done to me—trading me for drugs—get inside me. I just wrapped myself up in one more rock-hard layer of I-don't-care-'bout-nobody and sat in the living room, waiting for Daddy Mitch. I wanted to know for sure if Daddy Mitch be my real daddy or not. I never did ask before 'cause of how he had such a temper, but this time *I* had the temper, and I wanted to know 'cause I figured if he wasn't, I gonna run away somewhere.

Daddy Mitch come up and down the basement steps all day, dealing with strung-out addicts hot for their fix. He didn't know that I come home early, and when Mama Shell woke up, she were too groggy to care when I come home.

Daddy Mitch come up from the basement and took himself a break round 'bout five that night, and I were waitin' for him. I come right out and asked him what I wanted to know. I said, "Am I your daughter? Did you and Mama Linda have me?"

"Huh?" Daddy Mitch looked up at me from where he sittin' on the sofa.

I stood in front of him with my arms crossed over my chest, hoping he knew I meant business. I wanted a answer. "Are you my daddy or not?"

"What? You mean your birth daddy? You askin' me if I'm your real father?"

"Yeah. Are you?"

"Girl? Where you get a idea like that? Course I ain't your daddy. Don't you remember how we got you?"

I remembered, but I didn't say nothin'. Weren't nothin' could come outta my throat, anyways. I didn't think I could even breathe. I left without saying one thing and went to my room and put on the ladies and listened all night long and into the morning, and I didn't even think to hatch my running away plan, 'cause I didn't want to think at all. I got up the next morning and still didn't speak, and nobody minded. I went to school and didn't talk there, neither. I didn't talk and I didn't think 'bout nothin'. I just doodled on sheets of paper, spellin' out Leshaya over and over and puttin' little stars round my name and stuff like that. At the end of the day weren't nobody waitin' for me to pick me up, so I took a taxi same as usual. This time, though, the taxi couldn't get but halfway down my block 'cause of all the police cars jammin' the way. I got out the car and paid the driver, then walked down the street toward the cars, which mostly looked to be right in front of our house.

When I got up close enough to see what were goin' on, I saw the cops had Mama Shell and Daddy Mitch in handcuffs and they was leading them out to the cars. Behind them come more cops, carrying the bags and boxes of stuff from out the basement.

Neighbors I never seen before come out their houses and watched, so there were a good crowd and I was just one more in the crowd. I backed away and hid behind a tree, and I watched Mama Shell and Daddy Mitch ride off in the cop cars and the neighbors got out into the road and clapped and cheered behind the cars.

After everybody cleared away, I went on to the house. I stuffed what I could of what I owned into my backpack and a laundry bag. Then I searched the house for money and found a shoe box full of it in Daddy Mitch's room. Always were good things comin' in shoe boxes. It looked like Daddy Mitch robbed a bank there be so much money. I took all of it, putting some in my pocket, some in my backpack, and the rest I left in the shoe box I stuffed halfway down the laundry bag.

I called another taxi, and when it come, I told the driver to take me to the bus stop. I thought with the money I had, I could fly anywhere I wanted. 'Cept I couldn't fly to Tuscaloosa, where Harmon lived, and he the only person I knew to run to. Tuscaloosa weren't but a hour away by bus, so I took the bus, then took another taxi to the address Harmon give me at the mall.

The taxi left me off in front of a big house with lots and lots of lawn. It were dark out, but there was plenty of lights on the walk leading up to the house and plenty more lights on in the house. I took my time getting to the front door 'cause I thought maybe I be at the wrong place. Once I got to the door I felt too scared to ring the bell, so I went round to one of the windows and peeked in. I saw a pretty living room with lots of cushy-lookin' chairs with flower covers and velvety curtains on the windows, and it looked real warm and comfy in there. Didn't see no people, so I went to another window. I peeked in at the kitchen and saw Mrs. James wiping her hands on a towel and Mr. James and Harmon at the kitchen sink, doing dishes, and the little brother standing on his chair, holding his arms out for his mama to pick him up. I got the right house. I went back to the front and real quick, before I turned chicken and run off, I rung the doorbell.

Mrs. James answered it. She had the little brother in her arms.

"Hello," she said. "May I help you?"

I felt like I were in a store with Mama Shell. The salesladies was always following us around and asking could they help us. We always said no and looked annoyed at them, hoping they'd take the hint and go away, but at Harmon's house I smiled big and said, "I come to see Harmon." I held out my hand. "I Leshaya. I knew Harmon when he be at the foster home with Patsy and Pete."

Mrs. James stepped back to let me in. "Yes, Harmon said he met you a couple of months ago, at the mall in Birmingham. Come in, come in." Then she turned round and called to Harmon. "Harmon, someone's here to see you. Someone special."

Mrs. James had a singsong voice. I could see already why Harmon be happy living with her. And she were all dressed up like she just come from Sunday church, too.

I stepped into a large hallway that had a high, high ceiling with a gold-colored chandelier hanging down from it. The hallway had a pretty rug, too, with all these colors in it. It reminded me of a picture I seen of a stained-glass window once. I were afraid to step onto the rug, in case I had something dirty on the bottom of my shoes, so I stepped off to the side, set down my pack and my laundry bag, and waited for Harmon.

Harmon come into the big hall, and he saw me and ran right to me. He hugged me, and I wasn't scared no more.

"Leshaya!" he said, remembering my name. "Mama, it's Leshaya."

They brought me into a room they called the library 'cause it were full of books, and it had comfy chairs in it, too, only these were shiny-striped-covered, instead of flowers. I sat down, and Harmon sat next to me, and Mrs. James and Mr. James and the little brother they called Samson sat across from us.

Mrs. James said to me right off, "Leshaya, I hope you

can spend the night with us tonight," and her voice were so polite and friendly.

I said, "Yes, ma'am, I can. I come here to live. I come here to live with my brother, Harmon."

Mr. James and Mrs. James looked at each other, and they didn't know what to say, I could tell. I squeezed Harmon's hand and he patted my leg.

Then Mr. James said, "I think your own parents would miss you very much. If you've run away, I know they're worried about you. Could I call them and let them know you're here, safe, with us?"

"They ain't my parents, first of all, and second of all, they in jail. Maybe they in jail for kidnappin' me, and maybe they in jail for dealin' drugs. But anyways, they in jail, and my mama Linda put them there. She said yesterday she were gonna pay Daddy Mitch back 'cause he wouldn't hand her over no heroin, and she way addicted to heroin. She so addicted, she traded me off for it. But Daddy Mitch said yesterday he tired of the deal, and Mama Linda could take me back, but she didn't want me. So see, I don't got no parents. Alls I got in this whole world be Harmon."

Mrs. James said, "Oh my!" and reached out for Mr. James's hand. Little Samson come over to me and put his head in my lap. He had big eyes like Harmon, and his eyelashes be way curly. He were pretty, with pretty black skin, darker than everybody else's. I petted his head 'cause he were so pretty. He looked up at me and laughed, then he run back to his mama.

Mr. James said, "Well, we don't have to decide anything tonight. Harmon, why don't you show Leshaya the guest bedroom."

We all stood up, and Mrs. James asked me did I eat and were I hungry. I said I hain't eaten since noon that day, so she run off to the kitchen to fix me something, and Harmon took me up this wide, long staircase that had paintings hanging off the walls on either side of it. We walked down a long hallway to my room, and the hallway were wide enough to have furniture in it, tables and chairs and things.

The bedroom were like all the other rooms in the house, way big. It were so big, I think Mama Shell's whole house could fit inside the one room. It were so big, it had a sofa in it and a large chest for clothes and another one that opened and had a TV inside. It had a wide bed and the bed were gold. Harmon said it were a brass bed. I hopped on it, bouncin' and laughin', and I said, "No wonder you actin' so happy all the time, Harmon, livin' in a place like this. I think for the rest of my life I gonna be happy, too." I lay back on the bed and looked up at the ceiling. A brass chandelier hung down above me. The bulbs was shaped like candle flames. "Yeah," I said. "I gonna be happy the rest of my life."

chapter fifteen

I SLEPT LATE the next morning. Didn't have no school to go to and weren't no cars or trucks rolling past the house, wakin' me up, neither, so I slept. When I come down to the kitchen, were Mr. James sitting at the table, with little Samson standing on the chair next to Mr. James, saying he wanted a cookie.

When Mr. James seen I come awake, he stood up and told me to come on in and eat something. I sat down and ate me some toast and a orange, and drunk down a little bit of my glass of milk, but then little Samson spilled the rest of it all over the table and floor. I waited for Mr. James to smack little Samson upside his head, but he didn't never do it. He told the boy to fetch him a sponge and they both cleaned up the mess, Mr. James soaking up the milk, and little Samson standing on a set of steps set next to the sink and squeezing out the sponge. Back and forth little Samson go, and I sat watching, waiting for the smack that never come.

Then Mr. James told little Samson to run on and get out his puzzles and when he got them all put together, Mr. James would come out to the den and take a look.

Samson swung on my arm and laughed. Then he run out the room, I guess to do like Mr. James said and play with his puzzles.

"How old he be?" I asked when little Samson were gone from the room.

"He's three. His birthday was last week. He's full of mischief, that one, but very bright."

"You think Harmon be bright?"

Mr. James smiled and I saw his big white teeth. I had forgot about his big teeth. "Yes, Harmon is a smart boy, too," he said. "They're different, though. Harmon gets As, sometimes Bs, in school. He studies hard, but he's got a head for the arts and he's more spiritual. That Samson's going to be a scientist or a doctor. He likes puzzles and machines and computers. He's very curious."

I could tell how Mr. James were proud of both his boys, 'cause of the way he puffed up his chest and held his head so high up, and I thought how I wished someone be talkin' proud 'bout me like that. Then right away I thought how I hated Harmon. Were just this mean thought that come and fill my head, and the sad other thought went away.

Mr. James were starin' at me funny through his glasses, and I knew he had asked me something that I didn't hear.

"What?"

"I said, 'How about you? What do you like?'"

I sat up straight, actin' proud for my own self, and I said, "Singin'. Ain't nothin' better I like than singin'. I gonna be a singer like the ladies, Etta James and Ella Fitzgerald and Aretha Franklin and them. You know them?"

Mr. James laughed, and his laugh sounded like everything else in that house—happy, like music.

Before he could answer me, I asked him if he be related to Etta James, 'cause I always wanted to know.

He said, "No, but I've seen her. I heard her sing years ago. Is she your favorite?"

"Yes, sir. I sing most like her, I think. You really met her? What were she like?" I moved closer to him and touched his arm. He didn't seem to mind, so I touched it again. I wanted most to touch his eyes 'cause they what seen Etta James, but I were scared to do it. I were 'fraid he smack my hand away.

Mr. James said, "I didn't meet her, really. I just heard her sing."

"Same difference," I said. "If you watchin' her and hearin' her sing, you meetin' her. Wish I was alive back when she were singin'."

Mr. James took his arm away and blinked at me. "But she's still singing," he said. "She's still recording. Didn't you know that? Sometimes she even comes down here, to Muscle Shoals, to record her music."

I couldn't take in what he were saying to me. "What? What you say?" I asked. I stood up.

Mr. James nodded.

"She—she still livin'? She still alive? She singin'? Etta James? Etta James who sing "Stop the Wedding" and "Baby, What You Want Me to Do?" and "Tell Mama"? *That* Etta James? *My* Etta James?"

Mr. James laughed and nodded again. He nodded, and were like magic what it do to me. I just crumpled to the floor like all my bones gone soggy and couldn't hold me up no more. I cried. I cried with my face to the floor, and Mr. James tried to lift me up, but I be too limp for him to get a good hold of me. It seem to me that all my life my body been stiff with a kind of fear, a kind of waiting for something. It filled up my insides, that fearful waitin', but when I found out Etta James still be livin', my whole insides changed, everything round me changed. I could feel it. All the sharp edges of myself turned soft. It felt like the floor beneath me wasn't there no more. Felt like I were floating, and when I lifted my head to look at Mr. James, he were floating, too, first here, then there, floating.

Mr. James got down on the floor with me, and 'cause he so tall, it were a long way to go. He patted my back and said, "Shh," and "Shh," and after a while, I stopped crying and I sat up and I got a smile on my face.

Mr. James said he would find out if anyone knew when Etta James would be recording in Muscle Shoals again, and maybe he could take me up there.

I wiped my eyes. "Up where?" I asked. "Where be Muscle Shoals?"

"Muscle Shoals? It's right here in Alabama," he said. "Didn't you know that? It's up in the northwestern corner of the state, near Florence. Ever hear of Florence?"

I shook my head and my head were floating and so were Mr. James. We just kept floating.

"Muscle Shoals is famous. A lot of big hits have come out of there."

"Etta James in Alabama? For real? How you know that? How you know 'bout Etta James?"

"I did some legal work for a friend of mine who records up there. He knows her. He's a fan, too."

Etta James alive and singin' in Alabama! I weren't floating no more, I were spinning!

chapter sixteen

I KNEW IF ETTA JAMES could come to Alabama and record her music, then anything be possible. I could for sure become a famous singer my own self someday. I figured I could go to Muscle Shoals and sing for Etta, and she would help me get famous.

Mr. James said he wanted to talk with me about something else, but I couldn't hear nothin' 'cause my head so full of Etta James. I kept asking him questions. I wanted to find out everything he knew 'bout her and 'bout Muscle Shoals and her coming there and when he gonna find out if she coming again. "Maybe she through comin'," I said. "Maybe we missed her forever. How do you know we ain't missed her? You ain't makin' this all up, are you?"

Mr. James answered my questions, but he said he wanted to talk to me about something else. I weren't listenin' 'cause I didn't want to stop spinnin' and I knew what he wanted to say were serious, 'cause his voice were serious, and if I listened, the soft, fuzzy, happy feeling inside me would go hard again.

Finally, he took my hands and said, "Leshaya, please listen to me. We've got a social worker coming to the house in about a half an hour, and I think we should talk about it before she gets here so you know what to expect."

I pulled away from him and stood up. "You just said you was gonna take me to see Etta James. You just said it! Now you sayin' you givin' me away. You givin' me back to Patsy and Pete. Well, I ain't goin' back there to that ol' stink house. I'm goin' on. I'm leavin', and I can get to that Muscle Shoals on my own, 'cause I got money."

Mr. James got up off the floor, holding on to his back like it hurt to unfold hisself. "Leshaya, you won't be going back to Patsy and Pete, I promise you," he said.

"A promise don't mean nothin'."

"It does in this house," he said, and the way he said it, I believed him. I sat back down at the kitchen table, a nice, fat round table made of real wood that wouldn't give way when I dug my fingernails into it.

"Leshaya, they'll probably assign you a caseworker. Someone who will look after your interests. Someone just for you, who can see that you get the best possible care with the best family for you."

"But you the best family. You the best family I ever

seen. You be like *The Cosby Show* family. You ever seen *The Cosby Show* on TV? You be like that. And Harmon be here. He my only brother I got."

Mr. James nodded. "That's nice that you think of us that way, Leshaya. Let's just wait and see what the social worker has to say. Then we can go from there."

Mr. James talked smooth and real careful like that.

I didn't say nothin'. I looked round for something softer to dig my nails into besides the table. Weren't nothin' but my plate from breakfast with a orange peel on it. I got digging at that and Mr. James stood up and said, "Let me clear that away for you."

I watched him take my plate to the sink. He acted like he a woman the way he do the dishes and fix me breakfast. Daddy Mitch never touched a dish 'cept to throw it.

"How come you ain't at work? Don't you go to work?"

"Yes." Mr. James laughed. "I go to work. I'm a lawyer. I have my own practice." He finished rinsing the plate and set it in the dishwasher. He turned round. "I'm lucky. I have two offices, one downtown and one here at home. Today, I'm at home so I can be with you and Samson."

"Oh. So you got any more bread?"

"Sure." He got out the loaf of bread and set it on the table. "Have all you want. I'll get you some milk to go with it."

I smiled and dug my hand into the bag and pulled out a slice. I pulled off the crust and ate it. Then I rolled the rest of the bread up into a ball and dropped it into the sugar bowl they had sittin' out on the table.

"Oh!" Mr. James said, like he just touched something that give him a shock. He quick set down my glass of milk and reached for the sugar bowl. "We don't want to do that," he said.

"Yes, we do," I said back. "You ever suck on a ball a sugar bread before?"

Mr. James sat down with the bowl still in his hands. "Other people will want to use this sugar," he said.

"They can. I weren't gonna take it all. Go on, you have that piece and I'll make me another one. I can eat bread all day long."

"No." Mr. James set his hand down on mine that were already in the bag. "You have this one and I'll make my own."

"Really?" I took my bread ball out of the sugar and popped it in my mouth, and I were smiling so wide were hard to keep my bread tucked into my cheek.

Mr. James said, "Now, to really make this tasty, I'm going to spread some butter on mine."

"Butter! You'll ruin it!"

Mr. James had this teasing kind of look in his eyes, almost sneaky-looking the way he grinned and shifted his eyes while he were making his bread ball. He spread it thick with butter, tore off the crust, rolled it into a ball, and dunked it into the sugar. Then he popped it in his mouth, and I waited for his reaction.

"*Mmm*, delicious!" he said, and his mouth were still

chewing on the bread. He finished swallowing all of it and rubbed his hands together. He had skinny strawlike fingers.

"I haven't had sugar in years. That was superb. You're a good cook, Leshaya."

"But I didn't make it, you did."

"Ah, but you came up with the idea. That's more important."

I smiled and felt giggly inside myself. I made more bread balls and ate them. Mr. James said one be his limit, and he didn't have no more. He said I got a bottomless pit for a stomach the way I could put away all that bread and sugar. He let me eat all I wanted, so I kept eating. Then I saw my glass of milk just sittin' there gettin' warm, and I knocked it over on purpose. It got all over Mr. James's pants, and he sprang up from the table.

"You did that on purpose!" he said, and his brows was pulled tight together, he were so angry.

"No, I didn't. It a accident, I swear."

Mr. James clenched his face hard, so his jaw muscles poked out his face. His voice sounded choked when he spoke. He told me to get the sponge and clean up the mess while he changed his pants. And I did like he said, smiling to myself, 'cause he didn't hit me or nothin'. Were just like I be Samson or Harmon. Just like I be his own girl.

chapter seventeen

THE SOCIAL WORKER come, and she were a skinny white lady with a nose that turned up so much, every time I looked at her I could see straight through her nose holes to the inside of her nose. I couldn't keep my eyes on nothin' else when I looked at her, so I looked at the kitchen table and felt myself go hot in the face like I were blushing about it.

Mr. James went to check up on Samson and left me alone with the white lady. She wanted me to tell her my story of how I come to be at the Jameses' house and how my life been goin' so far.

I told her my life been goin' okay, but now I wanted to stay with Harmon. I wanted to live with his family. She kept writing stuff down on the paper she had on a clipboard, shaking her head and lifting it to look at me a second, giving me a shot of her nose insides, then back to the clipboard. She said to me, "Naturally, it's best if you live with a family of your own race."

I nodded. "That's right, and they my own race. My daddy were African American. My mama said so, so that's okay. You gonna be my caseworker?"

"Probably," she said, like she didn't care one way or 'nother.

"You gonna put me in a foster home and visit me all the time, like Doris?" If she been Doris I wouldn't mind seeing her every month, but this lady didn't look like she liked people at all. I thought seeing her all the time would be the worst kind of torture and I wouldn't take it if she said yes, but she didn't answer me. She shifted in her chair and wrote something down on her board. Then she said, "Why don't you let me talk to Mr. James now, okay?" She said it like I been keeping her from talking to him or something.

"I don't care," I said. "Do what you want."

I got Mr. James for her, and he told me to stay in the playroom and play with Samson while he talked with the social worker, but I didn't. I figured any child who got a whole playroom full of toys all to his own self didn't need nothin' else, and I wanted to listen in on what they sayin' to each other.

I snuck along and got myself to the bathroom just out from the kitchen and heard the social worker saying, "I can take her today and place her in a foster home, Mr. James, or you could act as a foster family—for a while at least, give her some time—then we'll find a more permanent solution for her. I have to tell you, though, she's almost thirteen years old and she looks much older. There aren't too many people out there wanting to adopt a child that old. The best we can really hope for is a foster home willing to take her indefinitely. And I think we'd better find her birth mother and take some legal action there. Leshaya said that the couple she lived with are already in prison. I'll look into that, too." Then the lady lowered her voice and I had to step out of the bathroom and peer into the kitchen to hear what she say.

"I should add that it's obvious from the lack of feeling expressed when she talks about her past that she's become quite detached from her situation—possibly an attachment disorder. Typical in her situation, though."

Mr. James shook his head. "I'm sorry, I'm not sure I follow you."

"Just keep your eyes open," the social worker said, tucking her clipboard under her arm and lifting up her head like she just the smartest thing in the world. "She's likely to steal things, possibly set things on fire. I've seen her type before. And keep an eye on your little one. Children like her don't care who they hurt to get what they want." She turned to leave and I popped back into the bathroom.

"Now, I'll be in touch soon," she said, "and I'll look into that prison story. For all we know it's all a lie. Children with Leshaya's background tend to make up the most atrocious stories, but we'll look into it."

That were enough! I sprang out from the bathroom and come charging at the pig-nose lady. "Weren't a lie! Weren't none of it a lie! You go on and check. You just check and see. And I ain't never leavin' with you, neither. If Mr. James say I cain't stay, then I'm movin' on. I can take care of my own self. I can sing! I can sing and make me lots of money. Ain't nobody takin' me nowhere I don't wanna go. Everybody always snatchin' me up and takin' me. I ain't goin' with nobody ever more. So you go on! Go on! Leave! Leave me alone!"

Mr. James come behind me and set his hands down on my shoulders, but they was trembling, uncertain hands. "Of course we want Leshaya to stay with us, for now," he said. "Thank you, Mrs. Weller, for coming. I'll be in touch with you later on in the week."

The lady backed her way out the kitchen door, saying, "Yes, we'll look into things and get back with you. Bye-bye, Leshaya. It's been nice meeting you."

That lady were phony to the end.

chapter eighteen

WE HAD ANOTHER meeting in the library that night, and Mr. James and Mrs. James said how they was glad I were staying with them for a while. Then they give me some rules I had to follow if I was gonna get along there all right. They said I had to go to school and do all my homework and take a shower every day. I said I been taking a shower sometimes twice a day for the past five years. I said they didn't have to worry, 'cause their rules be easy to follow.

Mr. James said that I would need to respect people and respect people's property and speak the truth and act polite.

Mrs. James said that I had to dress my age and look more proper, and I had to learn to speak correctly 'cause the way I spoke were hard for people to understand.

I said, "Okay, I will learn," even though, near as I could tell, more people spoke like me than them and they was the ones be hard to understand. I didn't mind 'bout none of their rules, though, 'cause I figured if I could just do those things, then I could stay with them and they could be my mama and daddy till I got famous. After singin' and being famous and meeting Etta James, weren't nothin' I wanted more than a mama and daddy like them who don't hit and who be the right color skin.

After our meeting 'bout all the rules, Mrs. James put Samson to bed while me and Harmon got out some Cokes and Doritos and set out the game Scrabble. Didn't never play no Scrabble before, but Harmon and Mr. James and Mrs. James, they all champion Scrabble players. Were like they all one team, the way they played and made me look a fool. I couldn't hardly get no points, and I had hard letters, like x and z, that spelled no real words. I kept putting my own made-up words down on the board and Harmon would shout out, "That's not a word! Get the dictionary!"

That damn dictionary! They was always lookin' in it to prove I be wrong all the time. They was ganging up on me, and the whole thing made my face go hot. I looked at Harmon studying his letters like it be so important, and I hated him. I hated him sitting between his mama and daddy like he king of the mountain. He put down the word *quark*, which I knew for sure were a made-up word, but they all ganged up and said it weren't.

I said, "Ain't no word *quark*. Get the dictionary!"

And Harmon grab the book all excited to prove me

wrong, and he flipped through and shouted, "Hah! Here it is!" when he found it.

I shoved my hand over the stupid board, messing up his damn *quark* and all the other words, and stood up. "Ain't no real word," I said. "That be a fake dictionary and I ain't playin' with cheaters. Y'all are cheatin'!"

I flipped the board off the table and run out the room.

A few minutes later Mr. James and Mrs. James come up to my bedroom and they say they be sorry 'bout what happened downstairs, and even though it were wrong of me to flip the playing board off the table, they was wrong to make me feel bad. They sat on the bed on each side of me and patted my back and hugged me, and I cried long past my hurt feelings gone away so they would keep hugging me. Then I asked where Harmon be at, and they said he were downstairs cleaning up. I hid my face back in Mr. James's chest like I were still upset, but really I were smiling to myself. Harmon were downstairs cleaning up and I were sitting in the middle of his mama and daddy.

Next morning we all ate breakfast together, and Mr. James and Mrs. James acted so lovey sweet to Harmon and Samson and just real polite to me, like I be company come to visit. Harmon stood at the stove making eggs and grits and bacon, and Mrs. James bragged on him to me 'bout how Harmon were such a great chef.

I said, "I can make eggs and grits better 'n him, any day."

Mr. James said, "I'm sure yours are delicious. We'll have to try them sometime." Harmon set my plate down hard, and Mr. James said, "Now, have a taste of that and see what you think."

I took a bite of the eggs and spit it back out on the plate. "Yuck!" I said. "Too much butter." Samson laughed and spit out his Cheerios.

Harmon took away my plate and divided it up between him and his parents, and Mr. James and Mrs. James spent the rest of the breakfast saying how every single bite were just delicious and scrumptious and other big words that meant yummy. I ate some bread, but Mr. James said I couldn't have it with sugar 'cause I wouldn't concentrate well in school. *Since when?* I wanted to know.

When we went up to brush our teeth, Harmon asked why I were acting so mean to him.

"Me? You the one always showing off at me. You waving how great it is you got a mama and daddy and how you get to cook the breakfast. Ain't you just a wonder?"

"I ain't showin' off," he said, and I smiled 'cause he talked like his old self and that made me feel better.

I went to school by myself 'cause I went to the public school. Weren't special enough, I guess, to go to no Christian private school with Harmon. He rode to his school in a car pool. I took the bus. The kids on the bus wanted to know where I come from, and I told everyone how I been kidnapped five years ago and were living in Birmingham and that I only just returned to my real family two days ago. That made me popular right away, so taking the bus weren't as scary as I thought it were gonna be.

Some white girls in my class asked me how come I talked the way I talked, and I said it were how I learned. One girl called me stupid, and a black girl called me "wigga," and I didn't know what it meant. Harmon told me later it meant I were a white girl who be into the African American culture. He said it weren't a insult, but I said it were 'cause I weren't a white girl, my skin just be real light. "I even got African American parents now, so that prove I be black," I said.

Harmon said I be crazy.

Wednesday night Harmon had choir practice at his church.

I told Harmon I wanted to sing real bad, and he said I could join the junior choir, 'cause the adult choir were for eighteen-year-olds and up. I weren't gonna sing with no baby choir, but I said I'd go with him, anyway. Seemed to me he just didn't want me getting in on his show. Anyways, he were just sixteen his own self and I told him so.

He said, "The only reason I'm in the choir is because I play the trumpet, and because I'm learning how to direct."

"That ain't no good reason. Only reason to be in the choir is if you can sing good, and I can sing real good, so I should be in the choir more than you."

Mrs. James told us not to argue about it no more. She said I could go and audition and let Brother Clevon decide which choir I belonged in. I could tell by the way she gave the eye to Harmon, she figured I'd get put with the babies and that would be that.

On the way to the church Harmon told me that Brother Clevon be a real grouch and acted like he owned everybody and didn't care what ugly thing he said to somebody when they singin' something wrong. Harmon said sometimes he even got people crying they so upset at what he said.

I told Harmon that no grouch gonna scare me or make me cry 'bout nothin', and anyway, I sing real good, so he don't gotta worry. "Don't you remember how good I sing, Harmon?" I said.

He said, "Yeah, I remember. But that was a long time ago, and Brother Clevon wants adults. You're not yet thirteen."

"I gonna be thirteen in a few weeks, and anyways, I got a adult voice."

Harmon shrugged like he saying in his mind, *Whatever. You ain't gettin' in, anyway.*

We got to the church and I looked out my window when we was pulling into the parking lot. I saw the biggest, cleanest brick building I ever seen. Harmon said the church had a cafeteria, a theater, and a gymnasium. Didn't sound like no church I ever heard of.

We got out the car, and right away I heard music coming from inside the building, only it weren't no gospel, were jazzy.

"Hey!" I said. "Listen to that. Why didn't you tell

me? This gonna be better than I thought." I started cross the lawn but Harmon grabbed my arm.

"That's not the choir," he said. "That's Mark's group. You don't want to get too friendly with them."

"Yeah? And how come?" I stood on the lawn with my hands on my hips, feeling the wet of the grass sinking into my little-girl tennis shoes Mrs. James got me wearing.

"They're part of the after-school program they have here for kids and teens who have nowhere to go. They're a wild bunch, that band. Preacher Walter lets them practice here to keep them away from the little kids at the gym, but they're trouble, anyway. One guy set off the fire alarm at the church last week."

"So?"

Harmon closed his eyes like my stupidness were too much to take in. He opened them again and said, "So there wasn't a fire and the whole fire department had to come to the church. It costs the taxpayers money every time they've got to go out, you know. What if there were a real fire somewhere else? They'd have all been here and someone's house would have been burning up."

I were gonna say something sassy to Harmon, but I heard the band behind us playing something new and I hushed to listen.

Without even thinking I turned away from Harmon and walked on toward the music. Harmon followed me and we walked across the lawn, following the sound. And I could feel myself walking to the rhythm, slinkin' along like a black cat looking for some leg to rub against. The music had that kinda sultry, mellow sound.

Round the back of the church, we come on the band set up on a porch that had glass windows you could prop open, leaving just screens. They was all playing their instruments, and they had their eyes closed or their heads bent low and their instruments up close to their bodies, and they was just feeling the music deep in. Me and Harmon, we standing, watching, and they didn't see us there. They went on playin' maybe ten minutes, and the music got smokin' and I got groovin' to it, moving my hips, my shoulders, my head, and Harmon said in my ear, "Look at you, thang."

I smiled and banged his hip with mine. Felt good to like Harmon again.

Then other choir people got showing up and the jazz band stopped playing, but I gave that Mark dude a look. He looked me up and down like he wanted to eat me up I looked so good. I went over to him to talk, and Harmon come with me.

Harmon said, "Leshaya, this is Mark. Mark, this is Leshaya." He said it like he was bored stiff and didn't care nothin' 'bout their music, but I smiled big at Mark and asked straight off did his band play anything for singin' to, like a Billie Holiday song or any good soul music. He lifted his sax up to his lips and played a quick scale, then said, "Sure, we play R & B, jazz, whatever. Why?"

"Why? 'Cause I can sing 'em. You wanna hear?"

The dude sneered at me like I be dirt-filthy all the sudden. He shook his head and turned away mumbling something 'bout how they don't need no girl in their band.

I called to his back and said, "I gonna be auditioning for the choir here. Why don't you stay and listen and see what you think?"

Mark looked back at me and shrugged, and him and the band went on and packed up.

Harmon told me to come on with him to the choir practice room and I did, but all I could think of were that band. I bad wanted to sing to something like that. If I could go to Muscle Shoals with a band backing me up, I just knew Etta James would say she gotta make me a famous singer right away. I could see myself dressed in a long evening gown—something white with gold sparkle trim on it—standing up on a fancy stage with lights all round and a band behind me and Etta sittin' in a seat in front of me and I'm just singin' out my soul for her. I could see it, just like that, in a flash in my head I could see it. I wanted it so bad it hurt and I had to push the flash thought away 'cause weren't no bread handy to soak up that kind of longing.

When Brother Grouch showed up, Harmon told him how I come to audition for the choir and the dude just shook his head and wouldn't take even a look at me.

I asked, "Why not let me sing for you before you say no?" and he said, "You're too young. Mrs. James told me on the phone, you're just twelve. Join the junior choir."

I knew Mrs. James weren't really believing me when I said I could sing, and there she went behind my back and told on me. Didn't matter, anyway.

I said to Brother Grouch, "But I got a good voice. What's it matter how old I be if I got a good voice?"

"It's not an adult voice," Brother Grouch said, like he know it all.

"How you know 'less you hear it? How you know 'less you give me a chance? Why you won't give me a chance, even?"

Old Brother Grouch turned round so his back were to me and he told the choir to pull out "His Eye Is on the Sparrow." I stood behind him, like a fool, and Harmon shrugged at me and joined the choir. Brother Grouch gave a signal for the lady at the piano to start playin', and since I knew that old song by heart, I sang out with the choir, only I sung louder. I sung with all my heart, like I be some kind of heavenly angel singin' for the Lord hisself.

The whole rest of the choir stopped singin', and Brother Grouch turned round and stared at me with such surprise in his face I wanted to laugh. I didn't, though. I belted out the chorus and filled the church with my voice. I saw that the jazz band come stick their heads in the door to see who be singin', and ol' Harmon, he just stood with his mouth hanging wide open like he was waitin' for a dentist to come along and yank out all his teeth.

When I finished singin', the choir people clapped and

Brother Grouch bowed to me, but I didn't have no use for them. I looked to the door, where Mark were standing, and I said, "So can I sing with your band?"

Mark were nodding his head like he thinkin', *Yeah, she be all right.*

I turned back to Old Grouch and said, "Too bad for you I too young, ain't it?" Then I marched myself off and went out with my new band.

chapter nineteen

I RODE WITH MARK and them to the Pizza Hut to grab some food while Harmon did his choir practice. We talked 'bout what songs I could sing, and this one dude they called Jaz got excited 'cause he wrote some songs he thought I'd be good at singin', and he give me a tape of his music to take home with me.

We rode back to the church after we ate and talked, but weren't no cars parked in the lot, so they give me a ride home.

Soon as I walked in the door all the Jameses jumped out at me and started asking me questions 'bout where I been and why didn't I call and let them know what I were doing, and I slammed myself up against the door, I were so surprised.

Mr. James said, "Didn't you understand Harmon was to take you home? He had no idea where you were."

And I lied and said, "But I told Harmon where I were gonna be. He just trying to get me in trouble."

Harmon sucked in his breath and said, "You're the one who's lying." Then Mr. James said that were enough, no arguing.

Mrs. James said, "In this house we let each other know where we're going to be so no one worries about us."

I said, "You was worried 'bout me?" And they said they was worried sick.

It felt good to think that they was worried sick, 'cause I seen how they liked worrying over Harmon and Samson and giving out hugs and sweet words. But seemed more like they was worried mad over me, 'cause I didn't get no hugs and they said I wasn't allowed to go off with Mark and them ever again.

I said that weren't fair, 'cause I didn't know 'bout the rule to let people know where you at. "And anyway," I said, "I already told you, I told Harmon I gonna go get something to eat."

Mr. James said, "We won't get into who said what. From now on you always let us know where you're going to be. But it won't be with Mark's crowd. We don't want you involved with them."

I said, "I just want to go to the church and sing. What be wrong with that?" I looked over at Harmon, who were standing with his head bent low so he could look careful at the dirt in his fingernails, even when there weren't no dirt to see. I said to him, "Tell them, Harmon, how I got to sing. Tell them 'bout that."

Harmon looked up from staring at his nails and shrugged. He looked back down at his nails.

I pointed at them and shouted, "You all against me! You don't want me to have any kind of dream." I cried real tears and they stood watching me. I said, "I gonna be a real famous singer someday. I gonna sing with Etta James. I got to sing." I got feeling hysterical about it, and I said again, "I got to sing!" I shouted it. "I got to sing! It's all in the world I ever wanted, and you won't let me 'cause you hate me. You can't wait to get rid of me. Well, you rid of me now, so there! I ain't stayin' when you all hate me."

I tried bustin' outta their circle, but Mr. James and Mrs. James held on to me, and they said I got to calm down and talk things out rationally 'cause that's what a real family does. Well, we went talking for hours into the early morning 'bout if they gonna let me sing in the jazz band or not. They said if I so bad wanted to sing, then I should be happy to sing in the choir, which I woulda been if I didn't hear the jazz band. If I sung in the choir, I'd just be singin', but if I sung in the jazz band, then I be practicing for Etta and for going to that fancy Muscle Shoals town to get famous—but I didn't say none of that. I said, "That music fit my soul. I belong to that music and it belongs to me." And that were true, too.

Finally, Mrs. James agreed I could go if Harmon be willing to take me and watch over me like I be some baby. So I got to go, and Harmon spent the time he had to wait for me doin' homework and giving me sad faces when he didn't like the saucy way I were acting with the band. I told him how I *gotta* act that way 'cause that's how the famous singers do it in Muscle Shoals. He said I weren't no famous singer, yet, and I said, "That just shows what you don't know, Mr. Harmon. I'm on my way more 'n' more every day."

Singin' and bein' in the band was all I could think 'bout. Didn't wanna go to no school or do no homework or clean no bedroom, neither. I just wanted to sing and sing and sing. Sometimes when I were practicing with the band, I sung like some kinda wild woman, and I knew I blew the whole band away. I could see lights dancin' in their eyes soon as I got singin'. I could feel the energy pick up in their playing, and when we finished a real red-hot song like that, we was all sweatin' hard. I loved it! Lord, I loved it like nothin' else. We would sing and play the whole afternoon away, and I didn't never notice the fading light or the storms sometimes building up in the sky, till the sky burst open and the rain flooded the muddy path to the main building of the church. I just felt the music like a storm inside me, and I sung it out 'n' wrung it out, and Lord, it were better than breathing. I didn't never want to do nothin' else but sing. I wanted to sing out my soul till it run dry.

And one time, after a real good session where I sung one of Jaz's quiet songs and we all got sad and mellow with it, I rode home silent with Harmon, and I thought, *So what if I cain't never get Harmon's parents lovin' me the way they do Harmon and Samson.* Didn't matter, 'cause I weren't gonna stick round much longer, anyway. Family life and rules wasn't for me. Soon as Etta come to

Muscle Shoals I were gonna take off outta there. I were meant to be a famous singer. I were meant to be travelin' and singin' and nothin' more. I knew, 'cause the only time I felt life be worth strugglin' with were when I be singin'.

One night when I were supposed to be doin' homework, I sneaked into Mrs. James's dressing-room closet and got me out her two evening gowns. I been in there before, just looking at what she got, and I seen them there, and I knew I'd have to come back and get them and try them on. They was long all the way to my ankles, and one were black and cut low in the back, and the other were white and come all the way up in the front with gold fitting round the neck like it be a choker necklace. The dress were almost just like the one I dreamed I would wear when I sung for Etta. Were so sexy looking on me the way it hugged my body, I couldn't stop looking at myself and thinking about that Jaz dude who be in the band.

Weren't just some of his songs that were hot. Jaz had a wild look in his eyes and a kinda hot-sauce energy when he moved that excited me every time I looked at him. His eyes was set real deep in his head, and his dreads and eyebrows hung heavy over them. He had a nose that looked like he used it to bust open doors, maybe some heads, but he had a pretty mouth with lots of curves to it. Were the prettiest thing 'bout his face besides his skin. He had the prettiest, sexiest skin I ever seen. Were more beautiful than Doris-skin, even. I just all the time wantin' to touch him and feel that warm brown skin on me.

When Jaz played his keyboard and I got singin', he could get me feelin' so wild inside it changed my voice and in some songs I had that raging, soul-bleedin' sound going that just heated up the whole band. Standing in that gown and watching myself in the mirror while I were thinking 'bout Jaz got me feeling so hot I had to lie down. I climbed onto Mr. James's and Mrs. James's bed and stared up at the ceiling. Then *boom!* The door slammed open and in come Samson and Mrs. James behind him. I sat up fast and got off the bed.

Mrs. James stood looking at me, and I stood looking back, and we neither one of us said nothin'. Samson come up and touched me and said, "Pretty." He pulled at my dress, and Mrs. James said for him to go on and get Harmon to give him a bath in the blue bathroom tonight, and Samson run back out the room, and me and Mrs. James stood staring again.

"I just wanted to see how I look in a dress like this, 'cause when I singin' I gonna wear a long gown and—"

Mrs. James waved her hand in front of her face, closing her eyes. "I don't want to hear it. Please, get out of my dress."

"Yeah, sure." I quick untied the back and pulled it off of me, and she turned her back to me while I got my own clothes on.

Mrs. James said, "When you've hung my clothes back up, meet me in your room and we'll talk."

When I got to my room Mrs. James were sitting in a chair with the pile of clothes and puzzles and stuff that had been in the chair, heaped on her lap. I grabbed some of it and said, "I were just gonna clean this up." I went to the closet and dumped it in there. Then I turned round again, and Mrs. James said for me to sit down. She said it like it hurt to push the words out between her teeth.

I sat down and Mrs. James's face went all soft and funny like she gonna cry all the sudden, and I looked away 'cause I didn't like seeing that kind of thing.

Then she out of the blue said, "Leshaya, you've been in my room before."

I said, "No, I ain't. Why you think that kind of thing?" I picked up one of Samson's puzzle pieces off my bed and tossed it a bit in the air and caught it.

"Some of my things are missing, Leshaya, and I believe you took them."

I tossed the puzzle piece up again and caught it. I said, "Weren't me. Probably Harmon took your stuff. He steals my things all the time. He were always doing that at Patsy and Pete's."

Were like she didn't hear me at all. She said, "Some of my jewelry—a ring and two necklaces—are missing, and a little black purse and a pair of black stockings. I'd like them back."

Well, how she could tell them things was missing when she had a whole mess of that same kind of stuff in her room, I don't know, but I said I couldn't say where them things got off to 'cause I never seen those things she talking 'bout before. I tossed the puzzle piece up again but missed catching it on the way down and it landed on the floor. I left it there 'cause Mrs. James were staring at me again.

Don't know what she were staring at, but I just waited her out, and finally, she give up and say I stole her stuff again. She kept pushin' at me to see if I would change my story, and then Harmon come in the room lookin' wet from giving Samson a bath, and when he saw what were going on, he stood leaning on the wall, with his hands behind his back, staring at me like I be some stranger he never seen before.

Mrs. James never yelled at me, and she didn't hit me, neither, but I could tell she were angry, anyway. She had a look so cross it 'bout made my heart stop dead, but I didn't change my story, 'cause I were stronger than her. So I won and she finally left, telling me first how I'd better clean up the mess in my room.

Harmon stayed in my room and watched me toss everything into my closet and pull up the top cover of my bed to make it look made up.

Harmon watched till I got done, then he said, "You'd better give her back her things, Leshaya."

I turned my back on Harmon and looked at myself in the mirror. Were a gold mirror like I figured they got all over the place in Muscle Shoals. I liked seeing my face with gold round it like that. I could see Harmon, too, in the mirror, standing all pudgy-faced and sad-looking be-hind me. I said to him, "What makes you think I took them things? Don't you trust me?"

"Who else would take them? We've never had any-thing disappear until you moved in with us."

Harmon's cheeks was all puffed out and his lower lip curled up like he gonna cry.

"Maybe they just gone missin'. Ever think of that?" I said, grabbing my hair and holding it back in a ponytail so I could see my face better.

He said, "My sterling silver pocket watch that's en-graved to me from Mama and Daddy is missing, too. I always keep that in my top drawer. I always know where everything I own is. Everything. I check every day to make sure my important things are still where I left them because I don't want to lose them. They're special to me, Leshaya."

I stood up and come over to where Harmon were standing, and I said, "Well, I never seen your watch or your mama's things. So anyway, how you think I'd look with black hair? Or maybe some dreads?"

Harmon's big old girly eyes filled with tears, and he said, "Stupid." He wiped his eyes, and I let go my hair and sat down on my bed. I didn't mean to be hurtin' Harmon exactly, 'cept he were always thinking he right 'bout everything. He so sure I stole his and his mama's stuff. They like a gang, the four of them. They like a special club. They all hang together on everything, and it were always against me. I hated every one of them.

Harmon said, "I'm really disappointed in you, Leshaya. You don't know how much you've hurt Mama. She's let you live here with us, and you go and take what belongs to her. Think about how she must feel. Think about us for a change, not you. You're always thinking about you—what you want, how you've got to sing so I have to drive you all over kingdom come, and how you should have the last slice of cheesecake, and go first when we all play a game. You're always thinking about yourself."

I jumped up from the bed and glared right at Harmon. I all the sudden hated him most. He sounded just like Mr. James talking and not like my old Harmon at all.

I said to him, "Yeah, I do always think 'bout myself. 'Cause who else gonna think of me first? Who else, Harmon? You think you so special now you got a mama and daddy. You think you so better 'n me just 'cause of that, but it don't mean nothin' at all. It ain't important. I already had four mamas, counting yours, and they nothin' special. Singin' what's special. You got no talent or nothin'. You cain't even play trumpet all that good. Nothin's more important than having a big talent and being famous. You just gonna be nothin' but something small someday, but I'm gonna be big. I'm gonna be real big. And I ain't waitin' round for it to happen someday. I'm takin' off soon, so you don't got to worry."

Harmon moved away from me and crossed his arms in front of hisself. He squinted his eyes mean at me, and I could see he were angry. He said, "What you say about having to look after yourself because who else will makes me feel real sorry for you, Leshaya. We're all really sorry for you. But you act so awful it doesn't matter how sorry we feel that your life's been so hard. You can't steal our stuff and lie about it just because you never had a family before. And we can't just let you do it because we feel sorry for you, either. And whether my life is big or small, at least I know it will be honest and good and full of the people I love and who love me. I don't need anything else."

"Then why you crying 'bout your stopwatch if you don't need nothin'? You just all the time trying to talk like Mr. James with all that love-and-bein'-honest talk. Wait till you through goin' to your fancy school that I cain't go to and you ain't in this fancy house no more and you out on your own, then see in the real world if you be talkin' 'bout love and honesty and blah, blah, blah!"

Harmon waved his arms. "I can't talk to you. You're always attacking. It's like you want to fight all the time."

"If you cain't talk to me, then why you here talkin'? So get out. Get out of my room, already. I don't want to be talkin' to you, neither!"

He left, but first he told me I'd better return the things I took if I wanted to keep living with them.

He closed the door behind him, and I shouted through the door, "Weren't gonna keep me long, anyways. So what do I care? Why do I got to follow homework rules and talkin' rules when I gonna be sent away soon, anyways!"

I waited by the door and listened to Harmon go into his own room and close his door. I knew he were gonna go back to doing his homework. He were always doing his homework or practicing on his trumpet.

I went over to the table and chair that was in front of the gold mirror and sat down. I picked up the hairbrush and held it like a microphone and watched myself sing real quiet. I pretended I be on a stage in Muscle Shoals with lights and gold all round me, and Etta James waiting in the audience for my song. My hands and knees was shaking like I really be there singin' for Etta James. I looked at myself good in that mirror and I told myself, "They don't want you here. You got to go. You got to move on now. Ain't no other choice."

chapter twenty

MR. JAMES AND MRS. JAMES called up to me from downstairs. They said they wanted to have another talk with me. I looked into the mirror and told myself to be strong. I had to be stronger than them all ganging up on me. I thought 'bout them things I took. Didn't know why I took them 'cept they was pretty. Each thing I took I found in a special place, all tucked in and cared for. Harmon's watch sat in a shiny silver sack lined with soft black velvet in the top drawer of his chest. Mrs. James's jewelry were in a fancy box that played music, and each piece were placed in its own special spot, and gold velvet lay all round them. Even the black purse and stockings was in a drawer with perfume-smelling packets inside. They was sittin' in the drawer like they so precious a thing, I just had to have them. And I knew when I were gone from the Jameses' house, all I got to do were look on them things and I'd remember how pretty everything were in that whole house. Anyway, they had a whole house full of pretty, they didn't need the itty-bitty things I took.

I were thinking 'bout all that when Harmon bust into my room and said, "Girl, get on downstairs. Didn't you hear them calling you?"

"Yeah, I'm comin'," I said, acting like I didn't forget but I were just cool and takin' my time.

I went on down to the library, and Mr. James and Mrs. James was sittin' together on their long sofa, holding hands. I stayed standing in front of them, telling myself how I be stronger than them any day, even if they do hold hands.

Right off they ask me 'bout them things that disappeared. I said I didn't know where their things be, but I would help them look.

Mrs. James told me to come sit by her, so I did, and she put her arm round me and said she would let me pick out something nice from her jewelry box that I could have, but it was real important that I tell her the truth and return her things.

I hung my head and got myself to crying. I said I didn't know what happened to her stuff, but I could pay her how much it cost so she could buy everything that she lost.

Mrs. James's voice got hard-sounding after I said that, and it made me go stiff hearing her talk. She said that telling the truth be way more important than the things that be missing. She said they weren't lost, they were taken from her.

I figured if tellin' the truth be more important to them, then they wasn't gonna miss what I took much, and what I took were way more important than tellin' the truth, to me. Anyway, I couldn't turn round and tell them a different story all the sudden, like, "Oh yeah, I forgot. I did take them things." Either way, they wasn't gonna keep me. If I lie, they say they don't want no liar livin' with them, and if I say I stole it, they say they don't want no thief in the house. If I stuck with what I said, then least ways I got to keep the pretty things. So when Mr. James told me I needed to tell the truth, I cried real hard and said, "Honest, I swear to God, I didn't take nothin'. Everybody always blaming me for everything. That social worker that come said it be my fault I got kidnapped. It always my fault."

I fell against Mrs. James and cried all out.

Mr. James said the social worker said no such thing. He said she would be coming to the house tomorrow to talk to me and if I wanted to, I could straighten that out with her then.

I lifted my head from off Mrs. James and looked at Mr. James. His face looked so cold at me, it made my throat go dry. He told me to go on and get ready for bed 'cause it were late.

I went up to my room and packed up my stuff. I didn't need no family, anyway. Didn't need no rules and people always ganging up, they always right and me always wrong.

When everybody went to sleep, I took my laundry

bag and snuck downstairs, going through the kitchen to get outside. I passed the phone on the way and set my bag down. I punched in Mama Linda's number, just to see. Maybe she were sorry 'bout what she done and wanted me to come see her. I might could stop by before I went on to Muscle Shoals and got famous.

Weren't nobody answer, though. I hung up the phone and dragged my laundry bag outside. I dragged it down to the end of the Jameses' driveway and hid it under a thick bunch of bushes. Then I went back to the house and went to sleep. Weren't no use runnin' away at night. I could just as easy run away in daylight.

chapter twenty-one

NEXT MORNING MR. JAMES drove me down the long driveway to my bus stop, same as usual, only we didn't say nothin' to each other. I could tell he hated me so much he weren't never gonna speak to me again. I got out at the bottom of the drive and held my hand on the car when it rolled on past me, feeling the warm metal of it. When Mr. James were gone from sight, I hid the pair of Mr. James's glasses I found on the seat in the car in my already stuffed-to-bulging backpack and got behind the bushes where I left my laundry bag the night before.

The bus come along a few minutes later, and the bus driver opened the door and waited for me. He waited there 'bout a minute or so, and I looked up through the bushes, watching the kids' faces in the windows, seeing them talking and moving round on the bus like it just another day and they don't got a care in the world. Then the door closed up and the bus driver went on.

I crawled out from the bush then and waited 'bout

twenty more minutes for the taxi I called up earlier from the house to come pick me up, and I got in with my laundry bag and backpack and rode away.

The taxi driver were real nosy, so I told him how I were gonna visit my aunt Doris, and I told him all about her, and I got so excited thinking 'bout the real Doris, I forgot I weren't really going to see her at all.

I guess he believed me well enough, 'cause he dropped me off at the bus station and went on. I dragged my stuff inside the station, but I didn't buy me a ticket to nowhere yet. I wanted to call Jaz first, figuring he might want to come to Muscle Shoals with me and watch me get famous.

I got his number the time he give me his new songs. I said I would take the songs home and practice but in case I had a question, I wanted his number. Never did get nervy enough to call till I were at the bus station, heading out of town. I knew his mama worked, and he didn't have no daddy, so I knew a weekday morning would be a safe time to call. But I forgot how early it were. My phone call woke Jaz up, 'cause he dropped outta school and he didn't need to get up so early. He sounded sleepy and hoarse in the voice.

"Hey, Jaz. It's me, Leshaya," I said, when he said hello.

"Shay? What time is it? Where are you?"

"I don't know. I guess it be round eight. I'm at the bus station downtown. You wanna go to Muscle Shoals with me? I'm goin' to Muscle Shoals."

"Why?"

"I'm gonna live down there. I'm gonna meet Etta James and I'm gonna sing. I can't sing and get famous in this poky town. Anyways, I got money."

"Yeah, how much?"

"Thousands. Thousands and thousands."

"For real?"

"Yeah, Jaz, for real. So, you comin'?"

Jaz took a second to think, then he said, "Okay. I'll go for a while. I was gonna quit my job, anyway. You say you got lots of money?"

"Lots."

"Where'd you get all that money? Never mind. I'll come, but I ain't leavin' my car. She's goin' with us. I'll pick you up. Give me an hour."

He hung up, and I dragged my stuff over to a chair and sat down to wait. I waited more than a hour and a half, but I didn't care 'cause I knew he were comin' and 'cause I were thinkin' 'bout Harmon, and that fill in the time. I weren't even at the Jameses' a month and, fast as that, me and Harmon wasn't friends no more. I thought 'bout that lots, but then I told myself it didn't matter. Didn't need no friend that always thinking he so special all the time. Anyway, I got a new friend. I got Jaz.

Jaz come on into the bus station lookin' round for me, and I called him over to where I were sitting. He looked at my laundry bag and said, "Man, you was serious, huh? What happened?"

I shrugged. "I didn't like the way the Jameses was

treatin' me. Besides, it's time I be livin' on my own. I'm grown. I don't need to be livin' with no parents watching over me, know what I'm sayin'?"

Jaz took up my laundry bag and heft it onto his shoulders, and, Lord, he had some fine shoulders. We walked on out to his car with me following behind, holdin' my hand in the back pocket of his jeans so we wouldn't get separated.

Jaz shoved my bag in the backseat of his little car. The car were a red Corvette, kinda old lookin' 'cause the red weren't shiny, but inside were black and real clean, and when I sat down in it, the seat gave a noise like a squeak. Jaz called his car Shirley or Shirl, like she alive or something, and I got such a kick out of that. I called her, "His Girl, Shirl," and Jaz thought that were a hoot.

"Yeah! My Girl, Shirl!" he said. He pushed down on the accelerator and we shot outta town, just like that! And the car roared like it happy to be racing away from Tuscaloosa. Jaz turned on some music—a tape of the band—and I started singing and so did Jaz, and we just flew on up to Muscle Shoals in His Girl, Shirl, like she were a jet plane. Seemed like it didn't take no time at all to get there, 'cause we sung songs the whole way, and I had my window down and so did Jaz, and I felt so free singin' and flyin' in our jet. Yeah, flyin' in His Girl, Shirl, goin' to Muscle Shoals to see Etta James and get famous. All my dreams was finally 'bout to come true.

chapter twenty-two

JAZ SLOWED DOWN when we rolled into Muscle Shoals, and all's I seen were nothin'.

"Where everybody be at?" I said, leanin' sideways and sticking my head out the window. "Where's the theaters and big studios? Where's all the fancy people?"

"Girl, what are you talking about? We're not in Hollywood. We're in Muscle Shoals."

"But Mr. James said all these famous people sing here—Aretha and Etta and the Rolling Stones. They made all those big hits here. Where all the rock stars and jazz clubs and stuff? This ain't the right place. This place is pokier than Tuscaloosa, even."

"This is the right place," Jaz said. "It just ain't Hollywood."

"Hollywood? Shit! This place the pits!"

Jaz rolled on through the nothin' street, and I were so

disappointed lookin' out the window, I couldn't speak. The shock of Muscle Shoals were so big I just kinda froze in myself.

Jaz pulled off the road at some hole-in-the-wall coffee shop and said, "Let's eat. You'll feel better after we eat."

I didn't feel like eating at no poky coffee shop. I wanted to eat at one of them fancy places with tiny lights and dark red carpets on the floors and music playin'. I seen pictures of them places and I thought Muscle Shoals were gonna be full of that kind of thing. But all this small town had was fast-food joints and nothing much else, 'cept the Tennessee River running alongside it, making fog. Were like we all the sudden stepped into some old-timey black-and-white movie. The whole town felt black-and-white.

"You sure this is the right Muscle Shoals?" I asked Jaz when we sat down to eat and I looked out the greasy window and saw the parking lot.

"Ain't no other," Jaz said. He waved at the waitress and said we was ready to order. Since I were paying, Jaz ordered most of the menu. Man, that dude could eat. I just had me a Coke and some bread I told the waitress not to toast. I made me some sugar balls and drank down the Coke, but I didn't feel much better. But Jaz felt great after he finished off his eggs and two orders of waffles and bacon and hashbrowns and toast and coffee and oatmeal and orange juice.

When we walked outta there, Jaz put his arm round my shoulder and breathed deep like he just owned the world, and I snuggled in close 'cause felt to me like I just lost it. How were I gonna get famous singin' in a place like this?

We made up our minds to find us a place to stay, so we asked some guy at a gas station where we should stay and if he knew where we could find the recording studio where Etta James sung or where people be playing jazz or blues music anywhere in town, and he said we come to the right place, 'cause he were a musician himself.

"I play guitar," he said. He took a cloth he had in his back pocket and wiped at his counter. "I got a band."

I said, "I heard all these famous people come up here like Etta James and Percy Sledge and Aretha Franklin. Where they be at? I don't want to sing with no gas station worker. I be a *real* singer."

Jaz give me a nudge like for me to shut my mouth, but I were too disappointed to act nice.

The dude behind the counter just kept wipin' over the same clean spot, smiling to hisself like I didn't say nothin'. "We made a CD," he finally said, like it no big deal, but really, I could see that he thought it was. "R & B stuff mostly, some jazz, some blues. You got a CD?"

"No," Jaz said, "we don't." He reached into his pocket and pulled out our tape of the band. "We made this, if you want to hear us."

The dude shook his head and kept wiping the counter. "Go on over to the Dragon, the Chinese restaurant a block away, and ask for Jimmy. He'll let you play your tape, and you can hear our CD. If you think you're any good, you can jam with us tonight. Jimmy will tell you. Go on over to the Dragon."

I were gonna ask again 'bout Etta James and where her studio be at, but then the dude said, "Jimmy'll tell you where Etta James records her music. He knows everyone. He knows all the greats."

We walked over to the Dragon and told this old bald-headed Chinese man who come up to us how we come lookin' for Jimmy to hear his CD. He said he be Jimmy. And me and Jaz give each other the look, 'cause who ever heard of a Chinese person calling hisself Jimmy?

He lead us through the dark red-walled restaurant to the kitchen and through the kitchen to a little office stuffed with shelves and papers and kitchen supplies. He said we could come inside. We come in, and a old Chinese lady with a million wrinkles on her face were sittin' at a desk, writing something on a computer, with a stack of them take-out cartons all flattened out, piled up on both sides of her computer. All that stuff round her made her look like some tiny doll, like my Doris doll, only Chinese. Jimmy said she were his wife, Elaine, and Elaine bowed her head at us and went back to writing like we wasn't there. Jimmy pushed a button on his CD player and music come on. It come out loud, and he quick turned it down even though he didn't have no customers out front or nothin'.

They sounded way good, just like professionals, but weren't no singin', weren't no Etta James. I asked him did he know 'bout her—where her studio be at and when she comin' back—and he said he would draw us a map of how to get to the studio where Etta James recorded "Tell Mama," but he didn't know when she be coming back down. He said, "Lynyrd Skynyrd here now. Jimmy Buffett be here next month, maybe, but no Etta James."

I didn't want to sing for no Lynyrd Skynyrd. I were thinking I didn't want to sing at all, I were so disappointed. Then Jaz pulled out his tape from his pocket and said for Jimmy to listen to our band, but I didn't pay much attention to any of that. I stared at the old lady with all the wrinkles on her face and thought how I wanted to go someplace and cry.

I heard Jimmy ask, "Who be singer?"

I lifted my head and said, "Me. I am."

He nodded and stared back at the floor. Didn't look surprised or nothin'. He listened through another tune, then he said, "You good here and there, but you uneven. Keyboard good, sax okay, but drums, trumpet, they weak. I like first song best."

Jaz nodded and said, "Yeah, that's mine. I wrote it."

Jimmy said, "I play differently if I do keyboard for that."

"What's wrong with the way we got it?" Jaz asked.

"Too smooth, too mellow. Listen to words. The sound all wrong. Come tonight and I show you. You jam with us. I draw you map."

Jaz got all excited 'bout that, like we was invited to sing with a famous band, but even though they was good, ain't never heard of them, so I didn't care none.

I let Jaz and him do the map thing. Weren't interested in maps, just singin', and I didn't like how this Jimmy dude said nothin' 'bout my singin'. It burned me good him sayin' nothin'. Right away I didn't like him, and I wanted to get back at him, say somethin' nasty.

When they got through with the mapmaking and they straightened back up from where they been hanging over the desk, I said to Jimmy, "Maybe you say that 'bout the keyboard being wrong 'cause you jealous 'cause we better 'n you and your band."

The old man bowed at me and said, "Maybe so. You decide tonight." He smiled like I paid him and his band a compliment, and that burned me even more.

The old man took us back through the restaurant, going through the kitchen first, where good sizzlin' smells was smokin' round the place and a dude dressed like a TV chef were shaking veggies in a pan as big as me. When we got to the front door, Jimmy patted Jaz's shoulder and said, "See you tonight—eight o'clock." Then he took my hand and held it in both of his. He bowed and said, "Young lady, it great honor to meet you. You have powerful gift. Use it well." He looked into my eyes, and I nodded, and it felt like I were making some kind of binding promise to him.

We left the dark restaurant and stepped out into glaring sunshine and walked back toward the car. My legs was shaking. Ain't never kept no promise before.

chapter twenty-three

THINGS JUST GOT worse that afternoon when we followed Jimmy's map to the studio where Etta James
recorded her music. Turned out it weren't nothin' to
look at. No great big building, no lights, nothin' shiny or
pretty or nothin'. Were a ugly building with ugly curtains in the ugly windows so you couldn't see into the
probably ugly studio. We couldn't even get inside 'cause
they was recording a group I didn't never heard of before. We drove on to a drugstore called Trowbridges,
'cause Jimmy said they had good chili dogs there, and Jaz
ate four of them while I had me another Coke and tried
not to let Jaz know how disappointed I still were 'bout
everything. How were I ever gonna get famous in a
dump like this?

We hung out the rest of the day at the river. I sat
sayin' nothin', but Jaz wouldn't shut up, 'cause he were
excited. He couldn't wait to jam with Jimmy's band, and
he said he loved how the town be like something outta

the past. He said it be like time stood still in Muscle Shoals, and I said that were exactly what be wrong with it. It done stayed still so long, it up and died.

Jaz said he were so turned on by the river and the atmosphere of the place, he just had to write 'bout it. He grabbed some paper and a pen from his car and started writing songs right there, with me sittin' next to him with my heart breakin'.

Some people come along on tubes, floatin' like it be fun sittin' on them tubes in the river. I saw them go round this corner of trees and disappear. I couldn't see or hear them no more. There they was all going along, all innocent like, till they round that corner, and I were just sure they found they come to the edge of that river and dropped off into nothin'. Even though I know from school how the world be round and not flat, I were just as sure as sure that they all dropped off the edge out there. So later, when I laid down in the grass, I made sure I were far enough away from that riverbed. Me and open water still wasn't friends, and I had to fight my thoughts hard not to keep thinkin' 'bout drownin'. I couldn't stop remembering that time I were drownin' in the Gulf of Mexico.

When Jaz got through with his songwriting, he lay back with me and sighed like he just so pleased with hisself. Then Jaz seen my arms and he rubbed at them. See, all this wet air were just hanging there all round us, invisible, 'cept on my arms. It left spit in the hairs on them. I liked him touching me. I snuggled up close to him on the grass, 'cause it were colder down by the water, and lay my head on his shoulder, my face facing in, looking at his. He run his hand up and down my back, resting it sometimes on my ass, and I got this achy thrill-chill feeling between my legs. Were the first really good feelin' I'd had in a long, long time.

WHEN SEVEN-THIRTY COME, we left the restaurant where we was eatin' fried catfish and hush puppies and headed out to the place Jimmy said for us to meet. Jaz had me reading the map Jimmy made, and I weren't good at directions, so I told him to take a right when I should have said left, and we didn't find out we was going wrong for 'bout fifteen minutes. Jaz swore at me and turned Shirl round, and we got right again.

We come to the house long after eight, and right away we could hear music. I looked up through the dark at the upstairs windows, and I saw the lights on. They glowed from the two windows like them soft lights be made from the sound of the sweet, warm music I heard playin'. Like it be music that make the lights come on— not electricity. I saw them lights and heard that music, and I started to feel a little better. We climbed up the stairs that run outside the building and knocked on the door. No one answered, so Jaz just opened the door and we walked inside. Right away I seen all these people through all this cloud of smoke, and there was all kinds of amplifiers and microphones and all this recording stuff. Ain't never seen a setup like it. The whole thing got me feeling jazzed. I just couldn't help myself.

We got introduced round, and turned out Jimmy were way older than everybody else, and the only Chinese dude. Seemed everybody treated him like a king even though he didn't play much, 'cause he were more like their manager.

They was all, like, in their twenties 'cept for me and Jaz, but even Jaz be almost eighteen, and they was all kinda dirty lookin'. Some had bare feet, and a couple of dudes didn't wear no shirts, and one lady guitar player named Colray or Tolray—didn't know which—she had a champagne glass tattooed on her boob, which you could see 'cause she wore her shirt so low you could see most everything.

They was a different kind of band from Mark's band. They noisy between songs and smokin' this and that and drinkin' beer and taking lots of breaks, and the guys was all flirting with me and the lady guitar player. They let me sing, and like always, soon as I got singin' I got feeling so fine. I forgot all 'bout runnin' off from the Jameses and how the town be so rinky-dink and how there weren't no Etta James waitin' for me to sing and weren't no way I gonna all the sudden be famous. I sung, and everything just felt all right again.

One dude howled when I got done singin' my soulful song, and that made me so happy I sung them one of my ragin' songs, and man, I got feelin' hot and steamy after that one. I got shakin' it, and all them in the band was touching me here, there, and everywhere, and passing me dope and I just kept shakin' it and drawing on the dope like I been doin' it for years, and I got feelin' better 'n' better. They said I had a powerful voice that gonna bring the house down like a earthquake. They gave me a beer and I drunk it, sure, like I always drink beer when I sing. I heard beer took getting used to, but I liked it straight away. It were like when I been sucking on my bread ball too long before I chewed it down and swallowed it. It had a bready kind of taste, so I had me another beer and sang with this dude who tucked his chin way in when he sung. I tucked my chin in, too, and got myself a cramp in my neck, so I didn't do that no more.

The singin' and jammin' was more fun than I ever had in my life. Dudes was coming up to me and playing in my ear and the lights from the ceiling flashed gold off the trumpets and gold off the sax—all those lights, all the sounds, my singin', the beer, the dope, dudes touchin' and rubbin' me, more singin', more beer, lots of great riffs back and forth from the drums to the sax to the keyboard—and me, I'm *hot*. I'm so hot I'm burnin' up the place. My throat's on fire, my body's lit, and I'm dancin' 'round the room and rubbing myself up on Jaz, then movin' and groovin' with Victor from the gas station, then moving back to center to sing like I never sung before.

We jammed all night, and when Jimmy left, round 'bout two in the morning, someone turned down the lights and brought out some big cookies, as big as my hand. Someone else passed round cocaine powder on a plate, and someone else brought out whiskey and more beer and cola and set it on a table with the cookies. Well, I tried this, and I tried that, all 'cept for the heroin someone were shootin' up his veins, then I puked in the toilet and lay on the floor. When they started playin' again, I stayed layin' there and let the sound come up at me through the floor, beating against my back—pound, pound, pound—like the drum hammer was beating the rhythms on my body and my heart were beating with the drums and the room were swirling and red lights was flashing till I got laughing, laughing hard till I cried. Then, don't know what come over me, but I got screaming. I screamed my lungs raw. Someone got down on the floor and put his hand on my mouth to stop my screaming. He got down on top of me to stop my screaming. He come down on top of me, and I stopped screaming. And I wanted what he give me, every bit of it.

chapter twenty-four

I WOKE UP CLOSE to noon, squinting in the sunlight coming through the two windows. I sat up and saw Jaz standing over me, with my clothes in his hands. He handed them to me and I put them on, staying under the blanket I had over me till I finished dressing. When I moved, I could feel my every bone and muscle were deep sore, and my head so tender, it felt like it made of glass and been shattered with a hammer.

Jaz bent over and reached for my hand. He helped me up and we tiptoed on out of the sour-smelling room filled with all the sleeping bodies. I looked back at the spot where I were sleeping and saw the body that been laying next to me. Couldn't see his face. Couldn't see nothin' but a lumpy, body-filled blanket.

"We need some coffee," Jaz said, when we got to His Girl, Shirl.

"Do we?" I said. I felt so sick, didn't want nothin' in me—nothin'!

He opened the door for me and I said I needed to lay down. He took out my backpack and laundry bag and let me crawl in the back. I curled up in a tight fist, hugging my knees close and hard, and closed my eyes to keep the sun from hurting them.

Jaz drove real slow for me and said he were sorry 'bout my hangover. He said, "Some wild night, huh?" And he said it like he weren't sure.

I said, "Don't remember nothin' 'bout last night." My voice were flat soundin', no music in it.

"You don't remember?" His voice still sounded unsure.

"I said I don't remember nothin'. Don't remember nothin' at all, so don't be talkin' 'bout it. Just get me that coffee."

I squinted up at him, at the back of his head, and I seen that his head be flat in the back. It look like he got no skull at all back there, just a hard plate covered in skin and hair. Seeing it flat like that, seeing his thick neck rising straight up out of his shirt, same width as his head, like his neck and the back of his head be one and the same thing, made me want to puke. I quick sat up and told him to stop the car 'cause I gotta puke.

I just made it out the door in time. Jaz waited in the car for me, and I were glad he didn't come out to hold my head or nothing or I woulda puked more.

I were finally ready to get back in the car, but then we heard a police car siren and Jaz said, "Shit!" and the car pulled up behind him with its lights flashing.

I stayed standing at the side of the road, kinda bent over at the waist, not feeling like it safe yet to stand straight.

The policeman got out his car and strut over to Shirl, with Jaz sittin' inside. He were 'bout to speak, then he saw me and he lifted his head and said, "You Leshaya?"

I hugged myself like I were feeling cold, even though the day were humid hot, and said, "Yes, sir, I be Leshaya. Why you want to know?"

He looked down and pulled something outta his back pocket. He brung it round and read something off it.

"Got some people looking for you. You know the Jameses?"

"Yeah, I know 'em. Why they lookin' for me?"

"They claim you're a runaway. That right?"

I looked off to my right, looking out at the blue day, feeling the hot sun on my head like it a knife cutting into the deep ache there. I didn't wanna deal with no fool cop. I didn't wanna face them Jameses, neither. I just wanted to feel that burning sun. Didn't want nothin' but the sun.

I didn't answer the cop, so he ducked his head into the window and said to Jaz, "You'd better have a good reason you're up here with this child. I'm gonna have to take the both of you in."

Jaz whipped his head round at me, giving me his fiercest look, then beat his hand on the horn like he wished it be my face.

Didn't matter if he were angry at me. Didn't matter if he found out how old I were. Didn't matter what that flat head thought no more. I lifted my head and stared wide-eyed straight into the sun and let it burn and burn and burn.

chapter twenty-five

WE GOT EVERYTHING settled at the police station fast enough 'cause Mr. James were there, and Jaz's mama come. Jaz had left a note telling her he gonna take me up to the Shoals, so that kept him from being a kidnapper. He 'bout freaked when he found out I were still a week away from bein' thirteen years old. His deep-in-his-head eyes popped wide open for that bit a news, and he kept swearing, and his mama kept swatting his head 'cause he kept swearing.

Mr. James took me home with him, and all he would say to me were, "Everything's going to be okay. It's going to be all right." I didn't think he were saying it for me as much as for his own self. It were like he needin' to pat hisself on the head over and over. Man, he looked a wreck.

I stayed at the Jameses' house two days. Didn't have to go to school or nothin'. They didn't talk to me much 'cause they was leaving all the talking for the social worker who were gonna come out to see me, but when they did talk, it weren't natural and happy talk. They was real careful with me and most of the time left me alone, even Harmon. All Harmon would say to me were, "You don't have a clue what we've all been going through, do you? Why do you have to screw things up all the time?"

I didn't know why I always screwed up, but I figured Harmon would understand that, but he didn't. He were on his parents' side. I were wrong and they was right. I were bad and they was good. I were mean and they was nice. And thing was, the more he thought I were mean, the meaner I felt inside myself. I didn't want to feel mean. I wanted to feel what I felt when I snuggled up to Jaz down by the river, and when that dude in Jimmy's band climbed on me to stop me screamin'. I wanted Harmon to hug me the way he used to at Patsy and Pete's. I wanted him to love me most again. So my last night there, I tried to get him to love me again. Soon as I figured everybody be asleep, I snuck into Harmon's room and climbed into his bed.

He had a panic attack when he woke up and found me next to him, especially when I brung his hand onto me and he find I got nothin' on. He sprung from his bed and told me I'd better get on outta his room fast before someone come in and find us.

I said I didn't care if they did, and I asked, didn't he want to make love to me?

Harmon didn't answer that, 'cause he were havin' a fit 'cause I were talkin' so loud.

"Shh, you're going to wake someone. Now, get out of my bed, Leshaya. Go on."

I got out real slow like I way tired and I let him see my body.

He turned away when he saw it and said, "Man, Leshaya, what's got into you?"

"Not you, that's for sure," I said, and I felt real mean inside me again. "Thanks for nothin'."

I left his room but I left my panties behind, in his bed, far under the covers where the maid gonna find it when she change his sheets.

NEXT DAY, THE SOCIAL WORKER lady with the piggy nose come and take me away. All the Jameses was glad to see me go, most of all Harmon.

I got took to some backcountry place to live with a lady named Joy Victoria. She were the best-named person I ever met, 'cause she smiled all the time. She were white and had brown hair and dimples in her cheeks and happy-snappy blue eyes and a square nose. She weren't skinny and she weren't fat, neither—just average. But all the time she happy and her voice like a song or a chirpy singing bird.

First thing she did when I come up to her door were fling it open and hug me like she knew me but hadn't seen me in a long time and missed me. Didn't care if she hugged me. I hugged her back like she my old friend, but I didn't feel nothin' inside. She told me to come in, and I

147

did, and I looked round the place. Her house be like a Hansel-and-Gretel house, not with candy all over it but with little glass things—glass dogs and giraffes and frogs and ladies in full skirts and flowers in their hands, and glass flowers in baskets and tied with glass bows and every kind of little glass thing. Most of them was painted but some was clear glass, and they sat in the windows and shined and gleamed, and the house felt like a happy house, a shining, singing house, so I were glad to be left with Joy Victoria.

She said I didn't have to call her mama. I could just call her Joy, so I did. Joy didn't take but one foster kid at a time, and she only took girls 'cause she only had one bedroom to share and it were small. The house were way out in the middle of nowhere, and Joy said she could take me to school, or I could be homeschooled 'cause she were qualified to teach all subjects up through senior in high school.

I said I didn't care, and she said that she would teach me, then, 'cause it were a long way to the school.

Joy had all kinds of talents. She been a nurse once, and a teacher, and even a policewoman. She ran a crafts business on weekends and a home computer business during the week. She had some goats outside, and inside, taking up all the spaces that don't have glass, were a big weaving loom and a spinning wheel and colors and colors of yarns and thick threads, and she did weaving and knitting and spinning and went round to fairs on the weekends, selling her stuff.

While I lived with her, I come with her to the fairs and ate myself some cotton candy and hot dogs and stared at all the people pickin' up stuff, then puttin' it back down again, not buying nothin'. Were lots of cranky kids at them fairs, too, no matter how full of sweets and lemonade their parents stuffed them.

Joy said she could teach me how to weave and knit, but I weren't interested. I told her I just be interested in singin' 'cause I had a big talent for that and weren't good with my hands.

Even though I wouldn't do knitting, me and Joy settled in real good. She said if I worked fast, I could be done with my schoolwork before lunch and have the whole rest of the day to do what I wanted. I did just that, school in the morning and singing to the trees and the goats all afternoon. And the work were easy 'cause she started me back a ways, since she said I were behind. Didn't mind doin' the work, neither. I just read stuff and wrote stuff in notebooks, and Joy come and check on me. She always right behind me, 'cause she weaving or spinning her yarn in the mornings, right there in the same room. She played music CDs while we worked, and it were Mozart music and Bach and Handel. Didn't mind 'cause it didn't have no words to bother me. I played her my tapes of the ladies, and she said we could listen to them every night with our dinner.

Joy let me eat all the bread balls I wanted till she found me yakkin' my food back up in her toilet. Then she thought maybe were the bread balls making me sick, so she said I'd better slow down with them. I did but I still got sick, and after a few days of that, Joy said I had to go to a doctor.

We had to drive a long way back to Tuscaloosa to see the doctor. Found out I were pregnant. I knew I were, anyway. I knew it the morning after that jam session in Muscle Shoals that I were pregnant, 'cause back in school when we learned 'bout how easy it were to get pregnant and how you could get pregnant the very first time you had sex, I knew that's the way it would be with me. So I didn't mind livin' for a while off in the woods with Joy, at least till I had the baby, then me and the baby could go on to New York City, where I for sure could become a famous singer.

Joy asked me, riding in the car on the way home again, did I know who the father be, and I said yes, even though I didn't. I couldn't remember what he looked like or even if he be black or white. That's when I figured out that my mama Linda always made up stories 'bout my daddy 'cause she didn't know. Just like me, she didn't know who the father really be. I decided right then that I were gonna give my baby a daddy and stick with my story. Weren't gonna change it every time I had a whim, like Mama.

After Joy found out I were pregnant, her smile at me got phony-lookin', but she still hugged me lots and said, "Poor, poor Leshaya," over and over.

But I didn't feel so poor. I wanted to have the baby. I were gonna do it right and love it all the time and not leave it nowhere or kidnap it or make it feel mean. I were gonna take it everywhere so it could keep me company, and I wouldn't never feel lonely or have that longing sick feeling in me no more. I were gonna love the baby and it were gonna love me back. A baby always loves its mama.

chapter twenty-six

I LIVED WITH JOY till the baby come, and she taught me lots about how to feed and clean a baby and how to hold it and everything else a mama should know, even though every time the social worker come to visit I were told I would have to give the baby away for adoption after it got born. I didn't say nothin' to the social worker 'cause I knew she didn't like me, anyway. She always looked at me like I be 'bout to snatch her hands off her arms, but I told Joy weren't no way I would let my baby live in foster homes and go roamin' round lost. No way I gonna let that lady with the pig nose take my baby.

Joy just smiled and said, "We'll see. That's a long way off from now." But I didn't trust her. She were showin' me how to take care of the baby and all, but she were agreeing with the social worker behind my back, and the two of them was planning on snatching it up soon as they could. I kept my eyes on Joy all the time, and I seen her making calls to that social worker and whispering stuff to her, too.

I had me a baby shower before I give birth. That's what Joy called it, but were more like a birthday celebration, really. I didn't mind. Joy made me a strawberry frosting cake and knitted me a red sweater, with pockets and a hood, and named a newborn goat Leshaya after me. I were afraid of the goats. I sang to them, but I didn't never touch them till Leshaya be born. Then I touched her and held her and pretended she my baby, and I sung her songs I made up that I knew was good. I were gonna be a really great mama, I could tell.

While I waited for my baby to come, I made secret plans for me and the baby to go to New York City, and counted up the money I took from Daddy Mitch's shoe box. Musta been ten thousand in there when I first took it, 'cause what I had left were $9,752.84! Every night I pulled my money from a pair of pants I never wore no more and counted it up. Then I wrapped the money back in the pants and stuffed it in my laundry bag and hid it away under my bed. Joy never did go inspecting my things the way Mama Shell sometimes did, so it were always just like I left it.

I made plans and got fat, and my tits turned to big heavy milk balloons, and my legs got swolled up, so when I did my schoolwork I kept my feet up on a chair. The rest of the day I were out walking round 'cause Joy said moving kept things circulating better, and Lord, I got restless doin' nothin' much 'cept waiting for that baby.

Joy took me to see the doctor regular, and he give me vitamin pills and told me to drink lots of milk and eat lots of fruits and vegetables, but all I wanted to eat were pizza. I wanted pizza for breakfast, lunch, and dinner.

First time I felt the baby kick, I wanted to kick it back 'cause it weren't funny at all. It made my stomach cramp. Joy said the cramping were gas, but I knew it be the baby and I couldn't wait till it come out of me.

Nine months come and go, and I so fat I can't walk round no more, and I don't want to eat or plan or do schoolwork or count my money or play with Little Kiddie-Leshaya. I just wanted the baby out! I yelled at Joy all the time and told her that her smiling at me when I be angry at her were pissin' me off good. Joy hugged me and asked me to sing her a song, but I didn't even want to do that no more. I told her if she wanted to hear a song, she could sing it herself, and she did.

Her voice were high and light and pretty. Her voice were real pretty, and I told her to stop singing, 'cause it made my head hurt. She didn't sing again, but it didn't help my head none. I could hear her voice singing in my head. I tried my own singing to get rid of her sound, but it didn't work. Her voice were real pretty, and she never used it. She sat in her knicky-knacky living room, weaving and tapping at her computer and correcting my stupid schoolwork, when she could be singing somewhere like New York City. She made me mad to think about it, and I got even more cranky, and good thing I did, 'cause one day when I were pitching a fit cause my legs hurt and my stomach were feeling awful and I were thinking 'bout Joy with the pretty voice not singing in New York and how I weren't gonna waste *my* talents, my water broke, and Joy said my baby gonna come soon.

I had the baby right there at Joy's house, and she were all prepared for it. She had all the equipment and supplies and knew just what to do, 'cause she were once a nurse, but she called the doctor, anyway, so he could be on the alert, case something happened.

Took eight hours and forty-five minutes to get that baby out of me, and Joy smiled the whole time and said I were doing great when I weren't 'cause my whole self were split wide open, and I didn't have nothing for the pain 'cept water and screaming. Lord, I ain't never, never, never gonna go through that again!

chapter twenty-seven

JOY CALLED THE SOCIAL WORKER and told her I had the baby—a girl, seven pounds, three ounces. The social worker said she couldn't get out to us till the next day, so I knew, as sick and tore up as I felt, I had to get out of the house with the baby right away so the pig-nose lady couldn't take my baby and give it away to some Patsy and Pete people.

We had a appointment with the doctor before the social worker's visit, so we packed up me and the baby, and I stashed my almost ten thousand dollars away in the knitted baby blanket Joy had made. I tucked the blanket and a bottle of formula and a change of clothes for me, and the stuff I stole from the Jameses, all into the diaper bag Joy also made me, and I added Kotex pads to wear in my panties like I had my period, 'cause I were still bleeding from having the baby. Joy didn't say nothin' 'bout how stuffed my bag looked, she just helped me get all of myself and the baby and the fat bag into the car. Then we rode out to Tuscaloosa.

One thing I always hated 'bout going to Dr. Bramley's office were how busy and crowded it be all the time. Were three other doctors sharing the office and waiting rooms and examining rooms. The day I run off with the baby, though, I were glad for how busy it were. One nurse weighed me and the baby and took my temperature, and another come in and said for me to change out of my clothes and put on the paper dress. Then she left and I left after her, and nobody noticed I walked out the back door and down onto the street.

I tried to act like I belonged there, walking with a baby in my arms, even though I were feeling way sick and kinda wobbly on my feet, and first coffee shop I come to I went in and asked the woman at the counter to call me a taxi 'cause I got to meet my husband for business and I'm late and my baby be sick.

She run off and made the call, and a lady come up behind me to pay her bill. She take a peek at my baby and said that she never seen a baby so tiny in her life.

"What a little darlin'," the lady said. "Is your husband Asian?"

I knew she were looking at the pretty skin, which looked like café au lait. I said, "No, my baby African American, like me."

The lady's smile fell off her face, and she turned her head to look at the lost-dog sign hanging behind the cash register. Then the woman who made the call come out and said it would be fifteen minutes or so.

I kept watch out the window, but nobody come running down the street looking for me. Probably didn't know I were gone yet. The taxi rolled up outside, and I said thanks and left and got in the taxi. Twenty-or-so minutes later, me and the baby was rolling up the long driveway to the Jameses' house.

The baby were fussy like it were hungry, but I didn't feed it till the taxi drove away. Then I went round to the back of the house, where Harmon once showed me a gazebo, and I sat there and fed my baby with the bottle I brung. I sung to her and patted her warm, sweet-smellin' head with my fingers, and she drank on the bottle like she starved to death. Now and then, she fell off the nipple and I had to put her back on or her face would flush red and her mouth would open like she 'bout to bust out crying. I never seen nothin' more helpless than her little self. She had a big mouth, far as I could tell, and no teeth, so you could see way to the back of her throat when she were wailing her teeny tiny wail.

I told my baby just how her life gonna be, and I think she were listening, too. I said, "Baby girl, you gotta stay with Harmon, just till the social worker stop lookin' for you. And it won't matter if she find you here, 'cause if she think you Harmon's baby, she'll see you been taken care of good by all the family and she won't take you away. But you don't got to worry none, 'cause Harmon, he gonna love you and take care of you the way he done me when we was little. Ain't nothin' like a hug from Harmon. And he gonna be your daddy, okay? But you just gonna stay with him for a little tiny bit, 'cause I be your mama and I gonna come back for you soon as I get on my feet good.

I set the bottle down and lifted the baby up to my face and smelled her deep. Her face and breath was warm and milky sweet and her teeny tiny hand brushed my cheek. I kissed her fingers and thought how my heart were gonna break if I had to leave her off at Harmon's. I stood up thinkin' I gonna run off with her into the woods or something, to hide, but when I stood up, I so dizzy and sick, I near dropped the baby out my arms.

I felt round for the diaper bag like I blind, found it and picked it up. "Let's go, now," I said to my baby. "Time for you to meet your daddy."

chapter twenty-eight

WEREN'T NOBODY HOME 'cept the maid when I rung the doorbell. I had to wait four hours till Harmon come home. I sat in the den with a glass and a pitcher of water on the table beside me, and I felt ripped sore between my legs and in my gut and sometimes like I gonna faint, but I kept drinking the water and sucking on the ice from the pitcher and going to the bathroom to see what were happening to me in my pants.

I tried keeping my mind off of feeling sick, by talking to the baby and thinking how it were gonna be, me tellin' Harmon this baby girl be his. He were gonna say no way it be his, and his parents would say, too, how it don't be his, but then they'll remember the panties I left in his bed and think maybe it do be his after all, and then they'll all be fussin'. Then 'cause they be like TV people, they'll take my baby. I pictured this over and over in the back of my eyes till Harmon come home.

When he come in the door, I heard the maid say to him, "You got a surprise waiting out in the den for you."

Then Harmon come trotting through the foyer toward me, and the maid called after him, "I knew those panties were gonna bring you trouble."

That stopped Harmon dead. "What?" he said.

I got up and come to the door and called out to Harmon.

"It's me," I said, grinning and feeling kinda shy. "It's me and our baby. Harmon, come see."

Harmon had his back to me 'cause he were turned facing the maid. When he heard my voice he whipped round and said, "Leshaya?" And he sounded so surprised, like he didn't never expect to see me again.

He looked at the baby I held in my arms and asked, "What's that?" And his big girly eyes blinked and blinked at me like he wanted to blink me and the baby away.

I moved toward him and he backed away. "It our baby, Harmon. Look at her, ain't she the prettiest, sweetest thing you ever seen?"

Harmon's chubby-face cheeks deflated like they balloons that just popped, and he blinked and he blinked, and I kept walking toward him, watching him blink, and when I got up close I saw tears in the corner of his eyes, and when I held out the baby and he lifted his arms, they was shaking.

"It be all right, Harmon," I said. "Here, take her. I cain't keep her or the social worker gonna come and put her in a Patsy and Pete foster home. Here, she yours now."

Harmon took the baby from me and opened the little blanket Joy knitted and put a finger on the little baby's hand.

"I named her already," I said, peering down at the baby with Harmon. Our heads touched, and Harmon lifted his and looked at me, still blinking, still tearing in the corners of his eyes.

"I named her Etta H. James. Ain't that perfect? Cain't you see her signing her famous autograph like that some day? Etta H. James. Etta Harmony James," I said.

A tear rolled down Harmon's sunken cheek, and he turned from me and walked away with the baby in his arms.

I figured I'd go sit back down and wait for Mr. James and Mrs. James. I knew there were gonna be a big fight coming with them two, and I were feeling way dizzy. I sat down and stared at the empty pitcher and wished I had me some more water. Maybe fifteen minutes later the maid come to the doorway and said, "The taxi's here. You can go now."

"But I didn't call no taxi."

"That's right. Mr. Harmon did. Now, you go on like a good girl."

I stood up. "That's it? I just leave? Don't gotta see Mr. James and have a talk or nothin'?"

The maid set her hands on her hips. "Taxi's waiting. Go on, now."

I left the house, just like that. It were so easy it made me nervous, like maybe Harmon didn't understand what I meant. I didn't get a chance to say how I wanted him to take good care of the baby. I didn't say how he were to never give her away for adoption or let anybody come take her. I just left the house and climbed my aching self into the taxi and didn't know what to think. The taxi lady tossed her cigarette out the car window and turned round to me. "So where we goin', sugar?" she asked.

I turned from the window and looked at the lady. Her orange head seemed to fill up the whole front seat of the car, and I could feel myself shrinking, shrinking till I were 'bout a inch high. The lady asked me again, "Where d'you wanna go?"

I said, "I don't know," and my voice were so tiny I knew she didn't hear. I said again, "I don't know!" loud so she could hear me. And I said it again, louder. "I don't know!" wishing she'd stop looking at me.

Finally, the lady turned round and shifted into gear, and we drove away.

chapter twenty-nine

THE TAXI DRIVER took me to a Holiday Inn hotel. I got me a room and had to pay the money for it before I even got to use it, 'cause I didn't have no credit card. The man at the desk wanted to know how long I gonna stay, and since I didn't know—'cause staying wasn't in my plans in the first place—I said a week.

I got me a nice blue-and-tan-colored room. Soon as I got in it, I fell on the bed, feeling soaking wet around the neck of my shirt and shivery like I got a fever. I lay on the bed and stared out at the room. Were a big room, with a table and a desk and two chairs and a chest of drawers, and all that furniture kinda danced, kinda floated. I closed my eyes to keep myself from feeling more sick, and I fell asleep.

I lay in that bed for two, maybe three days, with my body going hot and cold, wet and dry. I slept and slept all day, all night. Only time I woke up were to go to the bathroom, and that took every bit of energy I had in me.

I'd go drag into the bathroom and drop onto the toilet. Then, when I got done changing my blood-soggy pad and doing my business, I dragged myself back to the bed and fell back onto it.

I slept and dreamed dark dreams of drowning, but it were blood—all that baby blood that was still comin' outta me—that I were drowning in. All that baby blood comin' outta me and washing back over me, drowning me till I soaked the bed with my blood and sweat.

I kept moving to some new dried-out spot on the bed, doing it in my sleep without thinking, and waking up and finding myself staring at a different part of the room: the flower picture on the wall, the mirror, the desk, the door, the carpet.

After a couple of days, I got to feeling like for sure I were gonna die. My tits was so full, they hard and heavy, and were like all the milk filling up in them be a poison to my own body. I took off the Do Not Disturb sign I hung on the door. I pulled the sheets and mattress pad off the bed and balled them up together 'cause they was all stained with my sweat and blood, even if I did wear them pads I brung.

The maid come, and I hid out in the bathroom till she gone, 'cause I didn't want her saying nothin' to me if she found out how I messed up them sheets. When she left, I come out and seen she give me new sheets, all made up on the bed, and towels and more toilet tissue.

The maid come the next day, too, and she caught me laying in the bed. She looked at me fast the first time, then she looked again, and she said, "Girl, you don't look so good. You feeling all right?"

"I be sick," I said.

"I bet you need something to eat. You look real pale. Even your lips look white."

I sat up and looked across to the mirror and stared at myself, at my greasy hair that stuck to my head in knots, and at my dry sand-rough lips. My eyes looked big, and my head looked big, and I remembered Mama Linda all strung out on heroin looking like me, and all I strung out on were having a baby.

The maid stood looking at me in the mirror, too.

"I just had a baby," I said.

I told her 'cause I didn't want her to think I been on drugs and tell the hotel people. I weren't ready to get kicked out yet. Didn't yet know where I gonna go. I just wanted to lay down and die. I felt too sick for anything else.

The maid ordered me up some cinnamon toast and tea and orange juice from room service. She come back later to see if I ate it, but I couldn't get most of it down.

She looked sad about the food not being gone, so I said how I were gonna eat it later. She sat down with me, on the bed, like she got all the time in the world to talk to me, and she asked me, "Are you all right?"

I said how I be fine, I just need to sleep more, but inside I were sure I gonna die. Weren't no part of me that didn't feel in a fever and sore to the bone.

Then she asked about the baby, where it be.

I said the daddy got the baby. I said, "She with Harmon and his rich parents. Ain't nothin' gonna happen long as she with them."

And the maid said, "So, who's taking care of you? Why are you all alone at this hotel?"

"I'm a famous singer," I said. "Well, not famous yet but almost. I just split with my band, so I come here to crash, know what I'm sayin'?"

"Yeah, girl, I think I do," she said.

She patted my arm and told me I felt hot, and she said maybe I needed me a bath to bring my fever down. She went into the bathroom and run the water, and I dragged in shivering behind her and watched her fill the tub too high.

When it was way to the top almost, the maid stepped back from the tub and said to me, "You get in, and I'll be back in about an hour, after I finish my last set of rooms. Then I'll try to comb out your hair if you want. Why don't you wash it with that hotel shampoo? It's got a cream rinse in it that should help some."

I said okay, and she left me alone. I drained down the water 'cause it looked deep enough to drown in. Then I climbed in the tub. Felt like I were climbing into a bed of ice, were so cold. Took a long time till I got used to it.

I sat in the cool water almost the whole time she were gone, draining it and adding more water every time my fever heated it up, but I laid hot wash rags over my sore tits. They was swollen so big and hard, they hurt enough to make me wanna pass out. I lay back against the cool tub, with them rags on my tits, and tried to put my thoughts away from shivering and dyin'. I thought 'bout the maid and how she were too pretty for sweating away in a hotel, cleaning rooms. I figured she could be a fashion model 'cause she real tall and thin, with long, tiny muscles showing in her legs and arms, and she had dark black skin and a small face from the nose down to the chin, but big eyes and a big round forehead on top. She wore her hair way short like it be a crown on her head, and she looked beautiful, so beautiful, like a queen of royalty.

Before she come back, I took me a shower to wash my hair. And I left the drain closed so the tub filled up too high again. I quick got out the tub and put the panties and pants I been wearing all them days in the water to soak. Straight away the bathwater turned red. It looked like a whole tub of watery blood, so much blood, just like in my dreams. I turned the knob to let out the water and looked away till I heard the drain sucking at my clothes. Then I run the water cold again and soaped up my things and held them under the running water. I rubbed my panties together to try to get out the stains. Were stains on top of stains in them underpants, and I couldn't get none of it out. Weren't nothin' to do but throw them away.

When the maid come back she found me wrapped in towels, sittin' on my bed, with the phone in my hand. I quick set it down and she smiled at me.

"You got somebody coming to pick you up?" she asked.

"Ain't nobody home. Ain't been nobody at that number for years," I said.

The maid felt my arm. "You broke your fever. That's good." She reached in her pocket. "I brought you these Advil sample packets the hotel gives out." She pulled out the packets. "These should help."

I took them from her and said thanks. I laid them on the table by the bed. Then I picked up the spare change of clothes I had took out from my diaper bag, and I slow put them on. I already had my underpants on 'cause I still needed to keep a pad soaking up the birth-giving blood.

While I were dressing, the maid got me some water for the Advil. On her way back she seen my old underpants in the trash can, and she squatted down and pulled them out and saw I been bleeding.

"You need to get to a doctor," she said. "How long ago did you have that baby?"

I shrugged. "Five, six days. I lost track."

She dropped the panties and stood up. "Where are your parents? You have any parents?"

I were folding up my dirty shirt and bra real careful, like they be new and clean. I slipped them into the diaper bag, checking while I were at it to see that my money still be safe. I said, "My parents in prison. But don't need parents, anyways, 'cause I'm eighteen."

The maid shook her head and made a face like she real wise. "I know you're not eighteen," she said. "I'm just nineteen, myself." She handed me the glass of water, and I took the pills while she pulled a chair out from the table and brung it closer to the bed. She patted the chair.

"Come here and sit in this chair, and I'll comb out your hair. It's sure in a tangle, isn't it?" She pulled a comb out of the pocket of her maid's uniform.

I sat down careful 'cause everything hurt, especially my tits, leaking out milk, but weren't enough to give any relief.

The girl pulled my hair back gentle and combed it, bit by bit. I bent my head forward and let her pull at my hair, and it never hurt 'cause of how little-bit by bit she did it.

"Why don't you come home with me," the maid said after we been sitting saying nothing to each other for a while.

I kept my head bent and she kept combing.

"I don't even know your name, and you don't even know mine," I said.

"My name's Rosalie—Rosalie Brown." She brung her long hand forward over my shoulder, holding it like she wanting me to shake it.

I touched it and it were warm, and I saw how at the bottom of every fingernail, just around the bottom of the nails, were black skin even blacker than the rest of her skin—little shiny patches of the blackest skin. I held her hand and didn't want to let go.

She shook my hand in hers and asked, "What's your name?"

I held on to her hand. "Leshaya," I said.

"Leshaya? Leshaya what?"

"Don't have no last name. I be just Leshaya, like Odetta be just Odetta. Never had no last name."

Rosalie Brown squeezed my hand in hers, and I held on.

chapter thirty

ROSALIE LIVED IN a small green house, with a mama and three brothers and four sisters. All them living together bunched up in this little room and that little room—and there Harmon had a house so big, lots of the rooms stayed empty most of the time.

Rosalie's mama said welcome to me, but she pulled Rosalie off to the bathroom and wanted to know why she bringing another stray cat into the house. Seemed Rosalie every now and again bringing someone home from the hotel. Her mama didn't sound too happy 'bout me, and if I had anywhere else to go, I woulda gone right then, but I were dyin', so I just sat at the kitchen table and let everybody stare at me. We all could hear what the mama saying to Rosalie, 'cause no one else were talking.

Rosalie told her mama a bit of my story, about me just having a baby and being sick, and her mama come out the bathroom and put her hand on my head. "You feeling all right, baby?"

"No, ma'am," I said.

And she said, "I should say you're not! Rosalie? Why didn't you tell me? We need to get this girl down to the hospital."

I got to stay at Rosalie's. We spent all night down at the hospital, waiting—in this room with no air to breathe—for my turn to see a doctor. We sat with screaming babies and whining kids and cranky parents till finally somebody called my name.

The doctor seen me for two seconds, then give me all kinds of stuff to dry my milk out and cut the fever and stop my bleeding. He said he wanted to see me again in two weeks, but after that miserable night, I figured dyin' were faster and sweeter.

For all the days I lived with Rosalie and her family, I didn't remember but three of their names: Rosalie, 'cause she the one that brung me home; Myra, 'cause I went to school with her for a while; and Cliff, 'cause he were eighteen years old and way good lookin', like Rosalie. I kept my eyes on him so much, he told me to quit staring, but I knew he liked it, 'cause he were always standing in my way.

I slept on the floor in the girls' room. I had a thin mattress that rolled up and fit under one of the beds in the daytime. Every night someone woke me up—stepping on me to go to the bathroom.

I didn't hardly never see Rosalie, 'cause she worked at the Holiday Inn in the day and went to college at night. She studied every chance she could. Didn't never see a body work as hard as she did. Everybody had jobs to go to in that family—'cept the little ones and Cliff—and Rosalie's mama said if I were gonna live with them, I needed to get me a job, too.

Myra wanted me to work with her at The Coop, a restaurant college kids hung out at. I thought 'bout my baby, Etta, and told her I couldn't be wasting my time chopping veggies at no restaurant, I had to get me a job singin'.

"Know where I could get me a job singin' soul music, jazz, the blues, that kind of thing?" I asked.

"Talk to Cliff," she said. "He hangs out at a place that's got a band like that. They call themselves 'Kind of Blue.' I haven't never heard them play before, but they do some gigs round and about."

I were happy to talk to Cliff. He were sitting in the one chair in the house that weren't pulled up to the kitchen table. I come up to him, stepping over the two little ones playing at his feet, and sat on his lap.

"Girl, get off my legs. You're too heavy."

"I am not," I said. "I know you liking it. I know you like what I got."

Rosalie's mama called out from the girls' room, "That's enough of that kind of talk! Didn't we just spend another long day down at that hospital with you,

Leshaya, and you fussin' the whole time? You leave my Clifford alone!"

Me and Cliff laughed, and he set his hand on my thigh like he weren't even thinking 'bout what he was doing, but I could feel heat in his hand. It burned so hot it 'bout melted me down to the floor.

I leaned against him and said, "Cliff, I heard you know 'bout a band called Kind of Blue. I wanna sing with them."

He put his other hand on my lower back and rubbed it round and round. "Yeah? Well, they already got a singer."

I run my hand up his chest. "Not like me, they don't."

"Listen to you! You so full of yourself."

I nodded and moved his hand up higher on my leg. "I am 'bout singin'. Who they got, anyway? Cain't be nobody too good."

"That's what you think," he said, sliding his hand all the way up my leg.

"Yeah, that's what I think."

I made sure me and Cliff got on way good, and one day he took me to his friend Jay's house and told him I wanted to sing with the band.

Jay were a goofy-lookin' guy, with a long, hook nose and a big, big Adam's apple poking out his neck, and first thing Jay said was, "She's white."

And I said right back at him, "Ain't white, just light. And my daddy be blacker 'n you, that's for sure."

Jay stuck his goofy face up to mine, leaning over to do it, making me lean away 'cause he had marijuana breath. He said, "You're pretty, but you're pure vanilla, and we're not a mixed band. Anyway, we already got a singer." He stood up and flicked Cliff on the arm. "Man, what you doin' bringin' her around?"

"Bet you a thousand dollars I can sing better than whoever you got," I said.

Jay tilted his head at me. "Where you gonna get a thousand dollars?"

I crossed my arms over my chest 'cause that's where his eyes kept looking. "Singin'. I been paid plenty for singin', so you gonna hear me or not?"

Cliff nudged the dude. "Won't hurt to listen."

Jay squinted his eyes up at Cliff. "You got a thing goin' with her? This girl that hot natured?"

He didn't wait for Cliff to say nothin'. He put his arm round Cliff's shoulder and pulled me by the hand over to his other side so he could put his hand on my ass and squeeze it. Then he said, "Why didn't you say so? Sure, I'll give her a listen. Might be someone could use her, some other band or something, seein' how she's so hot-blooded ready to sing."

I weren't sure what all he meaning, but I knew he weren't just interested in my voice. I stepped away from the two of them, turned round to face them, and I said, "You the band that's gonna want me, and I'll sing for you, but that's all—period. That is, if *you* good enough, Mr. Ugly."

chapter thirty-one

DIDN'T TAKE LONG before Rosalie's mama sorry she took me in. She were all the time getting calls from school saying I been ditchin', and when she tried to get me to say where I been, I told her every kind of lie, and she knew it. She were smart, that one, but she liked the money I brung in, and that's what mattered most. Maybe if she didn't like it so much, she woulda seen I spent most of my time out with Cliff, but she liked being blind about the two of us. Seemed Cliff were the only one of mama's older children who didn't work regular. Rosalie said he couldn't concentrate well enough to hold down a job for long. His mind was always wandering off the job, and his body was always following.

I told Cliff if I got in Jay's band, he could be my manager. Every singer's got to have a manager, and since Cliff thought I were the most special thing to ever come into his life, I figured it would work out real fine, and it did—for a while.

Of course I got in Jay's band. The second him and the others heard me, Kamay were out and I were in. Kamay were the drummer, Tank's, girlfriend. After I come along, she still hung round the band, anyway, while Tank played drums, and now and again she played keyboard. Sometimes she sung with me or sung one or two songs on her own, but didn't matter to me, 'cause she weren't too good. Her bad singing just made me sound even better, and after I'd had my Etta, weren't nothin' my lungs couldn't do to a song. Were like givin' birth were some kinda strength-building exercise for the voice, 'cause, baby, I could melt it, burn it, smoke it, pipe it, and sink it! I could set the whole band on fire, the way I sung my songs. I could turn a mellow crowd into a rowdy mob and then set them down again, so mellowed-out they cain't walk. I mean, I had that kind of power.

We had a regular gig at Osprey's Downtown, where the college crowd hung, and on weekends we sometimes drove up to Birmingham or over to Montgomery to do some music at the clubs and bars they got there. I had me a fake ID so I could get into the clubs, but Jay give me a chaperone, anyway. My chaperone were supposed to see that I didn't get no alcohol or nothin'. His name were Bob, a fat white dude with long greasy hair and dirt under his nails. He always wore BO-smellin' T-shirts under stinkin' plaid shirts that wouldn't button over his big old belly, so he left them open. He were so tanked his own self, he never knew what I were dippin' into, and before I knew it, I were trying all kinds of junk and finding my "Ecstasy" in pills and thrills.

Cliff always come along wherever the band go, and he were more my chaperone than Bob. He tried to get me to be careful with what I took, telling me I shouldn't just grab at whatever going round, but I couldn't help it. And I were careful with the heroin, only smokin' it— never shootin' up. I told him he didn't understand the way musicians had to be. I said, "It part of what I got to do to get out there all the time and sing my soul out. Cain't do that without some kinda help. It too scary, know what I'm sayin'?"

"Yeah, baby, and I'm just sayin' be careful 'cause there's some bad junk goin' round." Cliff put his hand on my back and rubbed it 'cause he knew it got me relaxed. Man, that dude could melt me down fast.

"Okay," I said, turning round to face him and run my hands over his chest. "Okay, Cliff. I hear you."

But I didn't, really. I never knew what kinda wild I had growing in me all my life, till those two years singin' with Kind of Blue. By the time I were fifteen, I were out of Rosalie's house and me and Cliff was living in with Tank and his new girlfriend, Val. We shared us a couple of rooms in a house near the college campus. We wasn't there much, but when we was, we went crazy-wild. We got music screaming against the walls and windows, and crowds of people stuffed in on top of one another, bumpin' and grindin', poppin' and smokin', and whatever fell to the floor, we was down on our knees, licking it up like we was dogs.

We tore that place up good before the cops finally come one night and we got took down to the jail. Me and Cliff stayed there two nights before Rosalie come bailed us out, but she said it were the first and last time she gonna do it, and if she'd known I were gonna be so much trouble, she'd a left me in the hotel.

I had to spend at least half the money I stole from Daddy Mitch's shoe box to pay for what we tore up at the house, and that put me low on money, 'cause all the new money we made in the band got spent on junk and a place to sleep for the night.

Me and Cliff laid low for a bit, and Cliff give me another lecture 'bout watchin' myself, like I some kinda child.

I said, "Don't need to be watchin' myself with you round, 'cause you all the time doin' it for me. It gettin' so I cain't breathe on my own. We ain't joined at the hip, you know."

"I'm just caring about you, baby," Cliff said, using this so-sweet voice like he some darlin' pet. "You need someone to care for you. If I didn't watch out for you, you'd been dead by now. Didn't I keep you from going to the mountains?"

Every time Cliff wanted me to slow down and do what he say, all he got to do were bring up the trip to the mountains. Jay and Tank and some other people we didn't never know planned up this trip. They was all gonna camp out on top of Blood Mountain in Georgia. I weren't never in Georgia or in mountains, where Tank said you was up so high a cloud could come floating right past your nose. I was bad wantin' to go, but Cliff said were too many gonna be piled in the car already, and he thought it would be nice if him and me could be alone for a change. I planned to go on, anyway, and say nothin' to Cliff 'bout it, but when time come to go, they all took off before I got to the meeting place. The weather were bad going up, with thunderstorms and tornado warnings, and the car hydroplaned, flipped over, skidded off the road, and hit a couple of trees. Tank were the only one to survive the crash, and he said everybody were so high he were sure didn't nobody feel a thing when they crashed and died. His own leg got busted up bad, but he didn't know it till he crawled out the car and found he couldn't stand up.

I were gettin' tired of Cliff always bringing that story up in my face every time I wanted to try something new he didn't like. I said once to him, "That were just a freak accident. You just a scaredy baby. Cliff, you a scaredy baby, you know that?"

Cliff moved in on me the way he do, rubbin' my back and all, and said, "I am when it comes to you. You act like you don't care if you live or die, sometimes. But I care. You're my Leshaya, aren't you?"

"Yeah," I said, but I weren't too happy sayin' it.

A few weeks after we got out of jail, we hooked up with Marty and Marnie. Marty be the one who took over leading the band after Jay died, and Marnie be the college girl he were sleepin' with. We moved into a apartment with them.

Weren't long before we was up to no good again. I could wild it up all day with pills and dope and gettin' it on, and still sing all night long. My voice just got better and better.

Cliff said I needed to be on a schedule so I could come down off of whatever I be on after I sung. He said I needed to get me some sleep.

But I didn't never wanna sleep. I told him, "I got me a schedule. I don't do heroin till after I sing, 'cause it takes me down too far. That's my schedule. You don't like it, get outta my life."

I got to sayin' that kinda thing lots to Cliff after a while, 'cause I figured I were keepin' him in heroin and weren't no way he was gonna lose his honey pot. And Kind of Blue was gettin' known, too.

Marty got us a gig in Mississippi where all the gambling joints be. We stayed there a month, playing at the Shambala Club. And that joint were classy. The floors was picked up and washed every night, so you wasn't walking on sticky stuff and smellin' stale beer all over the place every time you come in the door, like most places we played at. Cliff didn't like the place, though, 'cause he were always having to watch me, and the place were too crowded to keep a good watch.

I were always slipping out with someone, leaving him

to come find me if he could. It got to be kind of a game with me. One time he come in on me and a guy named Leslie rollin' round on the floor of this hotel room together, and he 'bout broke the dude's neck before the guy cut himself free of Cliff's nasty grip and run outta there with only his briefs on.

I shouted at Cliff, "You don't own me! You cain't run my life the way you been doin'. You got to stop it now."

Cliff shouted back, "You get some clothes on!"

His eyes looked fierce, like he 'bout to break my neck, so I did like he said. I pulled on the first thing I come to, which turned out to be Leslie's pants and way too tight for me. It felt like my stomach cut in two pieces with them pants snapped in on it.

Cliff looked at me sucking in my gut. He flopped down on the bed and said, "What am I going to do?"

"'Bout what?" I asked, moving toward him just a little.

"About you. Why you doin' this to me?"

"Ain't doin' nothin' to you. I were doin' it to Leslie," I said, trying to make it funny.

Cliff looked up at me with his round eyes, and they was all watery. He said, "Do you try to hurt me on purpose? Is that it?"

I shrugged and searched the floor for my shirt. I found it and quick put it on. Then I let go my sucked-in stomach and the snap bust open on my pants. That felt lots better.

Cliff said, "Don't you love me anymore?"

I shrugged again and said, "Ain't never said I loved you."

"But you do. You do love me." He leaned forward and grabbed at my hand, but I stepped back, and he didn't get it. "Leshaya, I love you." His voice got trembling, his eyes all soft-lookin' 'cause they watery. "You know that, don't you? I love you. You're so, so pretty. I've never heard such a beautiful voice. You're special. You need special lovin'. Who else is going to love you the way I do? Who else is going to take all your abuse?"

"Lovin' the way I look and how I sing and holdin' me back the way you do ain't lovin' me, Cliff," I said. "Love is knowin' my soul, knowin' me deep down to my soul, and lovin' all the dark corners of it. Ain't nobody ever gonna love that, 'cause ain't no love there, not for you. Ain't no love for you in my soul."

Cliff left me and the band that night, and didn't never see him again.

chapter thirty-two

ON MY SIXTEENTH BIRTHDAY my life changed. The change maybe started sooner, but weren't till on my birthday that I knew it be happening for sure. That's the day I gone up to Muscle Shoals to record my first song. Mick Werner, a big-deal producer who goes around discovering people, caught our band playing in Mississippi that month we was there, and then he come to Tuscaloosa to hear us again. We noticed him right off 'cause he didn't look like no one else hangin' round the place: too clean-cut. He were a rich-lookin' dude, too, wearing a dark suit with a white T-shirt that didn't look like Fruit Of The Loom brand, and a shiny gold watch he were always checking. Even his bald head were shiny, like when you rich, everything got to shine. We saw Mick every now and then for three months. Then one night between sets he asked to talk to me private, and said he were interested in me making a recording for him.

"You mean me and the band or just me?" I asked.

He said, "Your band isn't a good fit. They're mediocre. They won't get out of the South with their sound, but you could. With the right music, the right backup, you could make it, Leshaya."

I dumped Kind of Blue right then, right there. Didn't go back to tell nobody I were leavin', I just quick packed up my stuff and left. At long last my day had come.

I went to Atlanta, Georgia, and stayed with Mick at the fancy Ritz-Carlton hotel downtown. He introduced me to Paul, lead guitarist in my new band.

Paul were twenty-one, just outta college, tall, white, and real serious-lookin'. He wore wire-rimmed glasses that made his eyes look like a couple of M&M's, but when he took them off, when he got tired, I could see he had big eyes—big, deep, mud brown eyes. For white, he were pretty good-lookin' behind them glasses, but he never laughed or smiled, and were a long time comin' before I ever seen him lay down his guitar.

Turned out Paul wrote music. He already had a CD out with just instrumentals on it. This time he had written a couple of songs that needed a singer, and Mick said I were the perfect one. He wanted me and Paul to record those songs together, and he'd see where that got us. He said he thought we could really go somewhere, make big money.

I looked over at Paul, who were sitting at the table they got in Mick's hotel suite, pickin' at his guitar and sucking on a grape he pinched from a big basket of fruit sitting in the middle of the table. The dude didn't even look up when Mick said we could really go somewhere. I wanted to jump up and down on the bed and kiss Mick's feet for what he were telling me, and Paul just picked at his guitar like he were making up a new tune right there in front of us. I figured the only thing that would get this dude excited be if his guitar be on fire, which were a tempting idea to me, but turned out something else got him excited—me, and not in a good way. Plenty of times I were ready to quit and go on back to Kind of Blue. Turned out Paul were a perfectionist. A pain-in-the-ass perfectionist!

Only way I could learn his song were if I listened to it, 'cause I ain't never learned to read music.

The dude were pitchin' a fit all over the place for that. "You can't read music?" he said, flopping his hand on the side of the chair like he just giving up on me right there, before even hearing me sing. He looked over at Mick with this give-me-a-break attitude, like he knew Mick made a big mistake getting me for his music.

"What's wrong with that?" I said. "Plenty of famous singers and guitar players cain't read music. Maybe you stink singin', so you don't want me to hear. Maybe you stink playin', too!"

Mick stepped in between us and settled us down and made Paul sing and play his song.

Didn't take me long to learn it, and I thought that would impress Paul, along with my voice, but forget that. He gone ballistic 'cause my phrasing weren't right.

Then my attack weren't right. I weren't giving it the right sound—the right *delivery*, he called it—and I weren't "coming in right on the beat."

"Lookit, asshole," I said, "give me a second or two to learn it, why don't you. I got the stupid-ass tune down, so give me a break."

"I could give you a year and you wouldn't have it!" He pulled off his glasses and glared at Mick. "She's not right. She'll ruin it. Look at her, she's high. She on something? I don't want her singing my song. She doesn't even get it."

"Who wants to?" I said. "All them big words and rooty-tooty poetry stuff. The song ain't got no soul to sing. How can I deliver what ain't there? All you got is a tune. You ain't goin' nowhere, and you nothin' without me singin' your song, but baby, you just lost your chance."

I tossed his rooty-tooty song on the bed, flipped my ass, and made for the door.

Mick hurried to grab me and pulled me back. "Don't be childish," he said. "If you want this, you'll have to work for it, both of you." He gave Paul the eyeball. "Leshaya, dear, you're good but rough. And you're right—you don't know the song yet."

"A hour ago you was actin' like I be the greatest singer since Billie Holiday, and now I'm shit? I don't gotta take this. His song be garbage, anyway." I tossed a look Paul's way, and he were studying his sheet of music like his own words be foreign to him.

"Yeah, you writin' your words like you in a English class," I said to him, going over to where he sittin'. "Stop trying to be so college, and get real. You got to get out of your head and into your heart." I stole that saying from Rosalie, who said Cliff were always in his heart and never in his head. Even though I stole the thought, it were true 'bout Paul. Were like he wore his brain on the outside of his head, the way you could see he were thinking too hard all the time.

Paul give me a hard stare, and Mick come up behind me and said, "All right, now, come on and sit down." He put his hand on my back and moved me toward the chair. He sat down between us two and looked at us both. "You two need each other to make this work. Now, I'll have someone come in to coach Leshaya, and Paul, you can look over your words tonight, maybe smooth it out a bit before you leave for the Shoals in the morning."

"The Shoals?" I asked. "He be goin' up there tomorrow? You said two weeks. You said in two weeks we be goin' up to record."

Paul said, "The band's going up tomorrow to record the rest of my music. We only need you for a couple of songs."

Mick nodded. "That's right. Paul will be back, though, and the two of you can practice together. Then, Leshaya, you'll go up with the band and record the songs."

I worked hard on those two songs, harder than I ever worked. The coach I had made me do breathing exercises, so I used my belly more, and had me change my dynamics—that's what he called it—so I weren't all comin' on strong the whole way through but had softer parts. He told me to think tender thoughts, like I were holding something precious, and that got me remembering my baby, Etta Harmony, and couldn't hardly sing at all, then.

Paul changed his words, and every day I practiced, I had to keep learning new stuff 'cause of how often he kept callin' from the Shoals with new changes for me to learn. But more and more the song were something that made sense to me and I could feel the tender come out of me without thinking of baby Etta. I could just concentrate on the words I were singin'.

We went up to the Shoals to record the songs for real two weeks later, just like Mick said.

Up there, we worked even more hard. There was nine of us in the band, including me—two girls and seven guys. Most of them I just met for the first time that morning, and a couple of them lived right there in Florence. I eyed them good to see if they be from the band I sang with last time I come up to the Shoals, but far as I could tell, they wasn't, and I were glad of that.

We got to the studio—nothing fancy 'cept the equipment and the photographs of famous singers hanging on the walls. I spotted Etta James's picture, and I got chills thinking she recorded right where I were gonna record. I asked about her, but no one at the studio knew if she were gonna come back anytime soon. Still, knowing she

been there—she been right where I were standing—
made me sure I could do it, too. I were gonna sing in this
small little town and make it all the way across the
U.S.A. That's what I told myself over and over, and I
tried to act nice to Paul 'cause he were part of my ticket
to ride, but weren't easy.

Paul still had to get everything just right. He
wouldn't let none of us take a break till we got it down
perfect, and he were still losing his temper at me and the
rest of the band. Sometimes he even tore up on his own
self, cursing 'cause he did something nobody in the
world would notice. Mick, back in the booth behind the
glass window, reminded Paul how we could dub over
the mistakes, but Paul wanted a perfect play-through, no
fake dubbing stuff. "If we went on tour with this, we
couldn't fake it," he said.

"And we couldn't keep stoppin' in the middle, neither," I said back. I were getting tired and so were my
voice. I hadn't hardly had nothin' to smoke or drink
since I got working with Mick and the coach, and things
was wearing on me. "You ain't never gonna be perfect," I
said. "Nobody's perfect."

He said back, "You won't get far with that attitude.
You're always going to settle for being average, aren't
you? You'll always just be average."

"Ain't nobody ever said I be average. Look to your
own self for average." I grabbed at his head of perfect-
cut hair and yanked on it good, and Mick and a couple of
other dudes rushed in from the booth to pull me off him.

Then Mick made us take a break, and too bad for Paul, 'cause everybody else were tired, too. While we ate bagels with jelly and drank down Cokes, we heard a playback of our songs. Away from the room we all had been crowded into, away from being so tensed up trying to do everything perfect, we sounded better than we knew. We sounded *hot*! Even Paul almost cracked a smile. Others in the band said I got it down solid. When I hit this one note I had to hold a long time, a couple of dudes said they got chills. And I knew what they was saying, 'cause so did I.

Lisa, the drummer, said, "Average, my ass. Nobody's average on this. This is superior."

Yeah, everyone were certain one song, "Clear Out of the Blue," were gonna be a crossover hit. Everyone 'cept Paul, of course.

chapter thirty-three

MICK HAD TO GET back to Atlanta that same day, but the rest of us hung out in Muscle Shoals and partied high at Lisa's place. She had her own house, didn't share with no one, and she were only twenty-three years old. Turned out she played drums on a lot of recordings of famous people but never played with Etta James. She said she met her once, though, and the lady were real nice. Were like Etta James be a shadow in my life, always just here, just there, meeting people I meet, but never can I catch her my own self.

I wore me a sexy black dress I stole from a Wal-Mart, back when I were living with Cliff and Rosalie and them, to Lisa's party. It were shorter and tighter than it used to be, so it showed off my body real fine. It had thin shoulder straps, with a bit of lace at the hem, like a slip, even felt like a slip. It were plenty cold outside that night, but at Lisa's house I knew I'd be hot struttin' round in my dress. I felt like I be Tina Turner in that dress.

Lisa had Greek food she ordered up from some place in town set out on a table, and I dove right into that, eating stuffed grape leaves and puffy pastry things I thought was gonna be sweet but turned out to be filled with cheese. Then I got mellow with a little dope and slinked around the room, rubbing myself up on this dude and that one, moving with the music Lisa had playing on her CD player, and all the while Paul were sitting off in a corner, Mr. Antisocial. I laughed extra loud, just trying to get him to lift up his head, but he were so into hanging over his guitar and picking at it, weren't nothing going to distract him 'less I fell into his lap, so that's what I done. I were careful not to bang into his guitar too hard, kinda coming at him sideways and stumbling into him. I laughed and looked into his eyes, and he said real mean, "Get off me!"

"What's wrong with you?" I asked him, still laughing like the way he said get off didn't mean nothin' to me. "You gay? Cain't handle a little female attention?"

"No, I'm not gay," he said. "Just picky."

"Well, don't you worry. You sure as hell ain't my type, neither."

I wiggled my ass at him and left, hooking up with Steve, who were glad to run his hands over my body. Didn't matter about Paul. He were so boring, just looking at him could put you in a coma. I told myself to just go on and ignore him, but the more I told myself that, the more I had to keep looking over at him.

I saw him set down his guitar and pull a pad out of his

pocket and write something on it. He hung over the little pad like he afraid it gonna get away from him. His bangs slipped out of place on his head and fell in his eyes, and he didn't never brush them away, just kept writing. Later I saw him back with his guitar, tapping out some rhythm, different from what were playing on the CD, then leaning over to make more notes in his pad.

A while after that I saw him eating a plate of food and drinking a Coke and talking with Lisa. The two of them talked close like weren't no one else around, and he got his bangs back behind his ears again so he were looking at Lisa real intenselike. Don't know why, but I bad wanted to know what they was saying. What kind of talk got Paul listening? I figured it had to be guitar talk, but they hung out a long time and Paul had put his guitar down and didn't even look at it once when he were talking with Lisa.

I wiggled my way back over in that direction with Steve's arms wrapped round me and tried to hear what they was saying, but I couldn't hear nothin' over the music. Steve said in my ear that we needed to be alone. "Come on," he said, "Lisa's bedroom's nice and quiet. Can't hear anything in here."

I didn't want to go, and that got me mad with myself. Why should I care what Paul and Lisa was saying? Why did I want to hang round listening and hearing nothin' but bad music when I could be rollin' round on the bed with Steve?

I grabbed Steve's hand and dragged him off to Lisa's

bedroom. We got goin' at it, burnin' up the sheets, but I couldn't get my mind on what I were doing. All I could think 'bout were working that song over and over again at the studio, getting it perfect for Paul—Paul wanting to do it one more time—Paul and his big hands. I didn't know I even noticed them hands. Big hands, with wide flat fingernails playing that guitar so fine. Right then, thinking 'bout those hands, I couldn't stand Steve being on me. Were the first time I cared one way or 'nother who I be doin' it with, and I couldn't take it. I pushed Steve off and he cursed at me.

"Think I'm gonna be sick," I said, struggling up out the bed. "Let's go eat something. Think Lisa's got any plain old bread laying round her kitchen?" I got my clothes back on, and Steve sat and watched me, stunned, like he don't know where he at all the sudden. I slipped my sandals back on and walked on out the room, leaving the door open so Steve could come on if he wanted.

When I got back to the party, Paul weren't sitting in his corner and Lisa weren't, neither. Both of them was gone, but Paul's guitar were there set back in the case Paul carried it in. I asked round where them two gone off to, and someone said they left.

I run out the house like I thought I gonna catch up with them. I checked out the cars, peeking in, thinking Paul and Lisa might be doin' it in one of them, but weren't nobody there. Didn't have no plan in case I did find them, and that were stupid, 'cause then I heard talking and looked up to find the two of them coming round the house, walking right toward me.

I jumped fast away from the car.

They both saw me, and Lisa called out, "You doin' okay?"

"Yeah, just cold. I were thinking of maybe gettin' a sweater out the car, but they both locked up. You got a key, Paul?"

"Ask Steve," he said. "He drove us here."

Paul didn't look at me when he talked. Him and Lisa kept walking past me, goin' round the house again.

I didn't know what to do 'cept stand there and watch them walk away. Then when I heard them coming back, I ran inside.

Steve were sitting in the corner, next to Paul's guitar. He were chasin' the dragon—sniffin' up heroin burning on a bit of foil. I went over and joined him and tried to forget about Paul.

chapter thirty-four

NEXT MORNING THE group of us going back to Atlanta got together, and everybody squeezed into Steve's car 'cept me and Paul. Paul were gonna drive the U-Haul truck with all the instruments in it, and I said I were gonna ride with him 'cause I ain't never rid in a truck before.

Steve said to me, "I was hoping you'd want to ride up front in the car with me."

Paul said to me, "The truck's no big deal. Anyway, I like being alone, if you don't mind."

I said to Paul, "Yeah, I do mind, and it ain't your truck."

I opened the door and climbed in, ignoring the both of them. Were a small truck, so Paul were right—wasn't no big deal—but I kicked off my shoes, put my bare feet up on the dash, and settled myself. I looked out the window, and I saw Paul hand a piece of paper to Lisa. She kissed him on the cheek and they shook hands. I rolled down my window, and I heard Steve ask Paul if he was gonna follow him or what.

Paul said he would follow, then he come round the truck and opened the door on the driver's side. He saw me like he forgot I were gonna be there and gave me a look like he already tired of me, and we hadn't even got on the road. He sighed big and climbed on in. He started up the truck and we was off.

We got riding along and I pulled me out a cigarette. Didn't really smoke 'cept at parties if someone give me one, but I had a couple I took off of Steve, in my pack, and since weren't no talking going on, I figured I'd light up to give me something to do.

"No smoking," Paul said.

"Say what?"

"No smoking."

"You ain't my health doctor. I can do what I want," I said.

"Out of deference to me, would you mind not smoking?"

"What you say? Man, I don't even know what you saying." I put the cigarette away and pulled out a stick of gum. "Can I chew gum or is that deference to you, too?"

"Be my guest," he said, waving his big ol' hand practically in my face. He changed lanes to stay up with Steve and said, "What's this guy doing?"

"What's wrong?"

"He's driving like we're doing the Indy Five Hundred. This truck isn't built for that kind of speed. We're losing him."

"Don't you know the way back?"

Paul give me a look like I be a bug workin' my way up his nose. "Of course I do."

"Then don't sweat it." I popped my gum at him and grinned.

Paul slowed down. "That must be your motto."

"Say what?"

"'Don't sweat it.' You don't care about anything much, do you?"

I shrugged and set my feet down on the floor, feeling for my shoes. "Don't care 'bout stupid stuff."

"You think making music is stupid?"

"That ain't what I said. Didn't say nothin' 'bout music. I care. I care 'bout singin', so just shut yourself up on that."

Paul didn't say nothin', and I sat burning up inside 'cause of the way the dude could get under my skin so bad. I wanted to get back at him, so I said, "You and Lisa was sure gettin' heavy last night, huh? You two get it on, or what?"

That got him. He pulled off his glasses and glared at me a full two seconds, at least, before shoving them back on his face and paying attention back at the road. "No, of course not. I just met her yesterday. Not everybody's a skank or...or a skeezer—is that what you'd call it? You know, I don't get you. You don't fit. Why do you talk the way you do, anyway? Who are you trying to be?"

"What? I just me."

"Who is that?"

"What say? Man, why don't you talk English so I can figure what you sayin'? Cain't get half what you sayin' to me—like I listening to a other language or something."

Paul wiggled in his seat like he got a butt itch. "I'm speaking English. I don't know what *you're* speaking— some kind of Afro-white speak you made up yourself, I imagine."

"Everybody make up what they sayin'. We ain't reading what we gotta say from a book, you know. 'Cept you. You all the time sound like you reading what you sayin' from a book. Your song were like it come from some bad poetry book, all them words nobody could understand."

Paul nodded. "You were right about that. I was trying too hard. I was showing off."

"Yeah, you was," I said. I put my feet back up on the dash, let my legs open and close, open and close.

Paul kept his eyes on the road and said, "What you said, 'Get out of your head and into your heart,' that was good."

"Yeah, I know music," I said, closing up my legs. "I don't write nothin' down, but I got me some songs I made up, too, and they good."

Paul give a quick look at me and he cracked a bit of a smile, so I could see his lower teeth and they was kinda crooked. "*You*—write music." He gave a *hah!* laugh.

"I said I don't *write* nothin', I just sing it the way I hear it in my head."

Paul were still grinnin', and I wanted to yank his pointy nose off his skinny face. "Go ahead, then, let's hear."

"I ain't singing for you."

"Uh-huh."

"What that mean? What that 'uh-huh' mean? You don't think I got me songs?"

He shrugged, and he still got that shit-eatin' grin on his face.

I sung him a song. I sung it quiet 'cause we was in a truck and 'cause most time when I sung my songs, it were to myself. Hadn't never done it for nobody else to hear before. Were a song 'bout Mama Linda gonna come back. Were a song 'bout waiting, and laying in the bed in the dark, hearing footsteps that weren't never there. I don't come out and say in the song were Mama Linda, don't say it were any mama I be waiting for, but that's what I know it be about, anyway.

When I got through with my song, I looked over to Paul and I seen I done it. I wiped that shit-eatin' grin clear off his face.

chapter thirty-five

ME AND PAUL stopped off at a Shoney's for lunch. He didn't want to stop there, 'cause he said it would take too long ordering food and sitting down. He wanted something fast he could eat on the road. I bad wanted a ice-cream sundae like I used to get with Doris, so I carried on 'bout how I hadn't never been to a Shoney's since I been little, and Paul give in.

While we was waitin' for my sundae and his hamburger, Paul pulled out some music-writing paper from his yellow girlie satchel he carried round with him, and started writing.

"Don't you never do nothin' but work?" I asked him. He held up his hand and shushed me.

I said, "You got hands like frying pans, you know that? I don't know how you can play guitar..."

Paul lowered his glasses and gave me a glare. "Would you please be quiet?"

He kept on writing even when his hamburger come,

but I weren't waitin' round till he finished, or my sundae be all melted and the chocolate be cold, so I dug on in.

Finally, Paul finished writing and he tore the page out from his notebook and handed it to me.

"What this be?" I said.

"Your song. The tune, anyway."

I took the paper and held it up close, looking at all them notes going up and down on the lines. "This really be my song?"

Paul nodded and didn't say nothin' 'cause his mouth were full of hamburger. When he swallowed, he said, "Here, let me have that a second. What do you want to call it?"

He held his pencil over the paper, waiting for me to say.

I shrugged. "'In Her Footsteps,' I guess, 'cause that be in the chorus part."

"Good." He wrote the title across the top of the page and put my name at the bottom, then handed it back to me.

I couldn't stop staring at it. I bad wanted to read it my own self, but I didn't say. I kept on with my sundae, still staring at the paper.

Paul put a finger on the paper and tapped it. "These five lines are called a staff," he said. "There are always five lines. See down the page? And this kind of dollar-sign thing is called the treble clef, and this kind of backward cent sign is called the bass clef. So you have the treble staff here—or the soprano staff—and the bass staff here.

I said, "Staff, treble cleft, and bass cleft."

"Clef," Paul said, "*c-l-e-f.*"

"Treble clef and bass clef," I said.

He said, "Right."

"But the notes," I said, and I pointed at the ones he drawn on the paper. "How come you got some smudged in, like here, and these here, they clear, and this note here be just like a circle?"

"That tells you how long each note is held. See the circle? You hold that for four counts: one-two-three-four." Paul beat out the counts on the tabletop. "You do it."

"Yeah, okay, that's easy." I beat out four counts just like him.

"Good," he said, and he cracked a grin and weren't no wiseass grin this time, neither.

We sat at the table long after we was through eating, and Paul taught me to beat out my whole song just by reading how many counts each note he wrote had. We was beatin' on the table and people was looking at us, but didn't neither of us care none—we was playing out my song.

When we got going on the road again, I told Paul I had lots of other songs, too, and he told me to sing him another one. I sung it and he said sing it again, so I did that, too. Then he said for me to get out his music paper and his pencil and I could write my own song down, and he would say what to write and what line to put the notes on. It took a lot longer for me to write it out than it did when Paul be writing, but I got it written down and didn't need to bother with no bass clef 'cause Paul said he could figure out the harmony later. I said, "So, you wrote harmony on this other song?"

He nodded and his bangs fell over his forehead.

"So, it like we wrote this together? Like we a team?"

"Well, you really wrote it. It doesn't take much to figure out a simple harmony, but yes, it was a team effort writing down this other one."

By the time we was just outside Atlanta, it were dark out 'cause we took so long at the Shoney's.

Paul got into the next lane to make a exit onto 285, then he asked, "Where do you live?"

"Don't live nowhere."

"I mean, where should I drop you off?"

"Don't know. Only time I ever been in Atlanta were last week with Mick at the Ritz-Carlton."

"Leshaya, where do you come from? Where is your home? Where were you living before Mick took you to the Ritz?"

Paul had this frustrated kind of tone in his voice like he wanted to bust my head open.

I said, "I don't got a home or nothin'. I were in Tuscaloosa living with this dude for a while, but we broke up. Cain't go back there."

"Are you a runaway?" Paul were startin' to sound stressed out. "Where are your parents?"

Oh man, I had fun with that one. I said, "Which parents you wanna know 'bout? I got Mama Linda, don't know where she be at. I call her up now and then, but she never home. Don't know 'bout my daddy, 'cause she ain't never said who he be. Then there's Mama Shell and Daddy Mitch, who kidnapped me, but I know for sure they in prison 'cause they dealin' drugs and they kidnapped me. Oh yeah, then there's my foster parents, Patsy and Pete, and the stink house in Mobile, and Harmon's parents—but they sure as hell don't wanna see me, 'cause I be way too much trouble for them to handle, and they all the time rattin' on me to the pignosed caseworker. Now, which one of them parents you be meanin'?"

Paul shook his head like he needing to shake something loose out of it, but he didn't say nothin'.

I said, "I'll just come home with you till I find someone else I can hook up with."

Paul 'bout shook his head right off his neck. "Oh, no. I'm not your baby-sitter."

"Say what? Ain't no baby! Damn! I give birth to my own baby already, so don't be callin' me a baby."

"Right. Look, I don't want you coming home with me. So, where can I drop you off?"

"Right here, then." I slipped my feet into my shoes and reached round to get my pack.

"I can't let you off on a highway!"

"Where's it matter where you let me off, long as you rid of me?"

Paul beat his steering wheel with the flat of his hand. "Okay!" he said. "Okay."

"Okay what? Okay, I can come home with you?"

"For tonight," he said. "Only for tonight."

chapter thirty-six

Paul's apartment were like none I ever seen before. At first when I seen the outside of the building so dirty-looking, with bricks crumbling out in places, I figured the inside gonna be run-down, too, but inside were all fresh white paint I could still smell in the hallway, and shiny banisters, and polished-up floors. Then I figured his apartment gonna be way neat, the way Mama Shell kept her house, 'cause of him being such a perfectionist. And it were orderly and clean, all right, but he had too much stuff for the place to really look neat and put away.

He had two more guitars, and a keyboard and amplifiers, two music stands, and a stereo and CD player, two big file cabinets where he said all his sheet music be stored, and everywhere was record albums, CDs, and books. He got a whole wood shelf high up to the ceiling filled with albums, and lots of more shelves with the books. He even had him a coffee table made out of stacks of books with a piece of wood set on top of 'em. He had a TV and a VCR, and a computer, too. All this were stuffed into one room, plus the furniture, like the couch and a couple of chairs, and then he had his bedroom. The room were dark and narrow with no window. All he could fit there were his thin bed and a built-to-the-wall shelf he put way up high 'cause were the only place to fit it.

I looked round the place a bit and said, "This all be yours?"

He said, "What? What's in the apartment? Sure."

"You read all them books?"

Paul shrugged. "I've read most of them. There's some I haven't gotten to yet, I guess."

I pulled a record off his shelf. He had labels marking off different sections on his shelves, like JAZZ and BLUES and RAGTIME and ROCK and CLASSICAL. I pulled one from the jazz section and looked over the cover. "Hey, 'Kind of Blue'!" I said. "This record be called 'Kind of Blue.' That were the name of my band I sung in."

Paul took the album out of my hand. "Well, this isn't your band. This is Miles Davis. It's probably where they got the name. It's a famous album." He slipped the record out from the cover, sticking his middle finger in the little hole in the record, and his thumb on the edge, and slowly, like he was praying over it first, put it on his stereo.

The sound were low, fat, and funky, and made me feel sexy in one hot second. I moved and grooved to the music, and Paul left me to it 'cause he were wantin' something to eat, but I didn't care. Didn't need nobody else. I could make love to my own self with that sound ridin' the beat.

Paul told me I could sleep on his couch for the night, but I didn't sleep, and I didn't need no drugs to keep me up, neither. Maybe the drugs from the night before hadn't wore off yet, 'cause I played his music all night long. I played Miles Davis three times. I played John Coltrane, Duke Ellington, Benny Goodman, Charlie Parker, and Herbie Hancock, from his jazz collection. I thought that each day I could listen till I had heard every song in his whole album and CD collection. I never heard such music, 'cept for what I got from the ladies. And he had all the ladies, too, even the old ones I hadn't heard from since I were kidnapped.

When it got to be in the middle of the night, when I were listening to Miles Davis again, I went to Paul's room and looked in at him sleeping. Couldn't see much 'cept the dark shape and shadow of his head, and I stared at that a long time. I stared and wondered what it be like to be him and know all he know.

Then this feeling come over me like I wanna bash in his head, so I left quick and looked round the kitchen for some bread. I couldn't find none, so I sat down on his kitchen floor and cried. Musta been the music making me cry, 'cause I hadn't cried like that in a long, long time.

chapter thirty-seven

NEXT MORNING, PAUL come out his room dressed in sweatpants and a undershirt, with his hair stuck up funny from sleeping on it. I were listening to Carla Bley and sucking on a chocolate Popsicle. He squinted a look at me and waved. Then he stumbled his way to the bathroom and I heard the shower turn on. Ten minutes later I were on my third Popsicle and listening to Anita O'Day, and he come back out, wrapped round the waist in a towel, and tiptoed to his room, a trail of steam drifting along after him. The dude had some hunkin' good shoulders and a sunken-in chest, like someone punched him there and left him a fist hole. It looked strange and I wondered how he breathed good.

When he come out his room again, he were dressed in a dark blue suit.

I come out from round the counter, which were the only thing keeping the little kitchen from being part of the rest of the apartment, and I laughed to see him all spiffed up.

"Where you goin' lookin' like that?" I asked.

"To work."

"What kind of work you do? You a undertaker?"

Paul tugged at the shirtsleeve under his jacket so it come down more. "I manage a music store. I don't usually have to dress like this, but I've got a meeting with the owners."

"Oh. Can I take a shower?"

"Go ahead."

I started stripping off my clothes, and Paul said, "Oh, please."

I threw my shirt at him. "Well, where else I gonna change if I don't got a room. Why you so 'fraid of me, anyway?"

Paul set my shirt on the counter and walked round to the kitchen cabinets. "You're underage, for one thing. For another, I'm not afraid of you: I'm afraid *for* you. You throw yourself at every guy you blink at. Someone could really hurt you."

Paul pulled a box of granola off one of the shelves and turned back round.

I stood naked with my hands on my hips and grinned big at him.

He closed his eyes and turned away, fishin' in the cabinet for a bowl. He let slip the bowl out of his hands, and it crash broke on the counter.

"Would you go on and get your shower," he said, using his hard voice and fumbling to pick up the broke glass.

"Ain't no one can hurt me," I said. "Ain't nothin' inside me that can feel that kinda pain."

"*Au contraire*, my dear," he said, turning and looking at me straight on. "Every note you sing is drenched in pain."

chapter thirty-eight

WHEN I COME OUT the shower, Paul were gone. I found the clothes I thrown off all folded up for me on the couch, and laying next to them were a book. Written in pen at the top right side of the book be my name, Leshaya.

"Do this be mine?" I asked, like Paul be still in the room.

The cover said *Music Theory and Composition for the Beginner.*

I opened it up, and already I knew everything on the first page, 'cause of what Paul taught me. I set the book down. I went to the only closet in the apartment and fished round and got me out a pair of jeans and a dark blue T-shirt of Paul's and put them on. The jeans was big and long but fit okay if I rolled them up and cinched a belt on. The T-shirt was big, too, and it had red writing on it: INTERLOCHEN CENTER FOR THE ARTS. I hugged myself in the shirt, put on some Albert Collins, from Paul's blues section, and sat on the couch with my book.

I fell asleep studying, not 'cause it were boring but 'cause I hadn't been to sleep for most of two nights and two days straight. When I waked up, it were quiet in the room 'cause the record I were playing been long over. I jumped up and put it back on again. Never did like silence, and anyways, I didn't hear much of the album the first time through.

I looked in the fridge for what to eat. I found me some cheese, so I ate that and went back to studying with my music book.

Sometimes when I looked up to think 'bout what I just read, I looked round at all the other books in the room and I kept thinking how in just another minute I were gonna have to get up and see what all them other books be about. But I didn't do it, 'cause I were 'fraid. I were 'fraid that them books be just like Paul—full of words I don't know and weren't never gonna understand.

When Paul come home that night, he come in almost bouncing with his walk. He had a sack of Chinese take-out food in his hands.

I said, "You actin' like you happy."

Paul set his sack on the counter. "Meeting went well," he said. "Plus, I got a call from Mick. We should be hearing our song on the radio before the end of the month, and he's looking into getting us a gig in New York City."

I jumped up and hugged him, and he hugged back

real quick, then set me away from him. He caught sight of my clothes and said, "Those are mine," real matter of fact, like he were just taking it in and not accusing me of stealing or nothin'.

I said, "Yeah. Look how far I got in your book." I held up the music book and showed him the paper I used to write stuff on. "See how I made my musical notes like yours. I remembered how you said you don't make little circles and fill them in, 'cause that were armerturish."

"You mean *amateurish*. Yeah, go on."

"So, see, I just did little smudges. And see, this is F and then A, then C, then E. That's the notes on the spaces, and here's E-G-B-D-F, for the notes on the lines."

Paul looked over my pages, kinda smiling. Then he said, "Now, why don't you play that over here on the keyboard?"

"Really? How do I do that? I kinda poked at it a bit today, but no sound come out from it, even when I turned it on."

Paul went to the keyboard set up beneath a couple of windows and showed me how to hook the keyboard up to the amplifier. Then he showed me where to find middle C and how playing notes on a piano be just like saying the alphabet, only there be only seven notes that just play over and over, A-B-C-D-E-F-G and A-B-C-D-E-F-G.

He helped me curve my fingers just right when I pushed them down on the keys and showed me how I should hold my wrist up off the board the way a professional do. He said, "Might as well learn it right the first time." Then when I done it a couple of times, he said I were just a natural at music.

I played it again, then skipped every other note like he said to do. Then I played notes C-E-G all together, which be a chord, and it sounded so pretty, didn't wanna never stop and eat no Chinese food. My stomach were upset from all the cheese I ate, anyway.

That keyboard were wild. I could make it sound like a whole band be in the room playing A-B-C-D-E-F-G with me, just by pressing a button on the side.

Paul let me play at the keyboard while he heated back up the Chinese dinner. Then he said I had to come eat so I would have energy to learn more things the next day, and he said I needed to get good sleep, too, so my brain would work right. "You can't learn well if your body isn't fed right and you don't get enough sleep," he said. And he didn't say nothin' all night 'bout me leaving and living somewheres else.

chapter thirty-nine

I DIDN'T EAT MUCH of my food. First I didn't want to
'cause I wanted bad to get back to playing the keyboard.
Then I knew that I were gonna be sick, so I left the table
and hung out in the bathroom half the night. Getting
sick tired me out so bad I fell asleep till I got sick again.

Paul got up with me and wrung out a washrag for me
to wash my face with, and he said it were probably all the
drugs I been taking going through my system.

I said if that be true, then he better get me something
to sniff fast 'cause I didn't want to be sick no more. Were
worse than when I were pregnant.

Paul got scared I were gonna sniff on his shav-
ing cream or something, so he come with me back to
the couch and waited in the dark with me till I fell off
asleep.

Next time I waked up, I saw Paul come out the bathroom with the towel round his waist and that fist hole in

his chest. I watched him go to his closet to get out clothes from it, and I got up from the couch and snuck over behind him. When he turned round I touched his chest.

Paul sprang back from me like I touched him with a hot fire poker. "What are you doing?" he said, and his voice had a real angry sound to it.

"What that hole be? How you breathe with that deep ditch in your chest?"

"I breathe fine. I was born this way. There's nothing wrong with me."

"'Cept that be ugly."

"Thank you very much." Paul turned away from me and went for his bedroom.

"Rest of you be okay, though," I said to his back.

He turned back round at me. "Every body has its flaws."

"Mine don't," I said. I lifted my arms up like I wearing some fine evening gown, but I were still wearing his big Interlochen T-shirt.

He couldn't see nothin' of my body, but still he said, "Hah! I beg to differ!"

"What's so wrong with the way I look?"

"For one thing, you have that drug addict's pallor."

"Ain't no addict. I'm just kinda sick. Haven't had nothin' since the party."

"Well, your skin's yellow."

"That be 'cause I part African American."

"Impossible." Paul turned away and laughed on into his bedroom and shut the door.

I stomped over to the door and pounded it. "Ain't impossible if it true, asshole!"

He called out. "You have hair so blond it's almost white, and it's baby fine, and your eyes are blue. *And* your skin, when its color is not drug induced, is most likely so fair as to be translucent. You haven't a single African American feature."

"I got full lips and a great ass!" I shouted at the door.

"My lips are fuller than yours, and your ass isn't so great."

"Didn't think you was lookin', anyway, Boy Scout." I went from the door and sat down at the keyboard. I turned that sucker way up, flicked on the band sound button, and played my chord.

Never in my life did I see a body shoot outta his room as fast as Paul come flying outta his. He grabbed my hand off the keyboard and shook my wrist so hard, I expected to see my hand dropped off at my feet.

"*This* is *not* a *toy!*" he said. "You treat my belongings with respect or you get out of here. Everything in here I worked hard to get. It's my whole life in here—my whole life—and I take my life very seriously. You understand?"

I blinked up at him. His hand were still gripping my wrist. I said, "Yeah, I understand good. Never met nobody else before who know what I been feelin' all my life 'bout singin'. Never met nobody loved music way I do, 'cept you."

He let go my hand.

I looked down at the keyboard. "Sorry what I done. Won't do it again. It give me a headache, anyways."

Were the first time I ever felt sorry 'bout anything.

chapter forty

I WERE GOOD and sick all of that first week I stayed with Paul. I knew if I had me some heroin or something, I'd be fine for a time, but didn't feel like leaving the apartment and goin' on the hunt for it. Paul said if I got into drinkin' or drugs at his place, I were outta there fast. I told him threats didn't work on me, so if he wanted me gone, he had to just go ahead and say so.

One night, when I come awake and seen him staring down at me, I rolled onto my back and asked, "How come you lettin' me stay here, anyways?"

He went over to his keyboard and poked at it. Then he said, shrugging his shoulders, "I like teaching you music. You catch on fast, and you're so into it. I like that." He turned and looked back at me. "You're such an enigma to me. I can't quite figure you out."

I thought *enigma* be a bad insult, but he said it meant I were like a puzzle to him. All I could think of when he said that were them puzzles little Samson James had in his playroom. I liked to sneak them things up to my room at Harmon's and play with them, so I guess Paul were kinda playing with me. He were playing at being a music teacher, but I didn't mind 'cause I were learning good stuff, so I didn't take no drugs or nothin'. I didn't want to get kicked out.

Anyways, for a long time, I were just too tired and too sick in my stomach to do nothin' but hang over the toilet, then go sleep on the couch. The second week, though, I got to feeling lots better, but I still never left the apartment, and I still went asleep a whole lot, too. Paul said my sleeping rhythm were off 'cause I were sleeping in the day and up prowling like a burglar all night long and that I needed to force myself to stay awake more in the day till I got a good rhythm going again. Didn't tell him how I never had a good sleep rhythm in the first place, and I didn't say how it weren't just old drugs running through me making me sleep so much, neither. I were sleeping all the time 'cause for once I didn't feel like I had to keep lookin' left and right to see what shit be coming at me next. Ain't never known what safe felt like 'cept when I been close to Harmon or smokin' heroin. Heroin were the only thing wrapped me up close and safe, till I come to Paul's.

Safe at Paul's felt warm and snuggly, laying on the couch under the sun yellow blanket Paul give me, and good music playing, and Paul coming home with hot food to eat. And even though Paul were real picky about everything, including something called MSG that he didn't want sitting in his food even when it be invisible, Paul felt safe, too. He were always thinkin' 'bout me, wanting to teach me music stuff, and giving me vitamins to take every morning. He let me wear his clothes, and he made sure I be comfortable sleeping on the couch, and especially, he let me play all his music.

After I got over being sick, all I wanted to do were sleep nice and warm and deep, then wake and play music on the keyboard, or study my theory book and listen to records. Paul give me more and more music books to learn. Seemed there weren't no end of learning, when it come to music. Of course I couldn't keep all his books he give me—they was just for borrowing, he said—but I liked how he trusted me. He trusted me with all his stuff and never checked to see what were missing from his apartment, neither.

For the next couple of weeks, I worked on learning music, and when Paul come home from work, we first ate whatever dinner he brung home, then he checked over what I learned in my theory book and what I worked on in the piano books he had got out for me to play. Sometimes after that, we went to a friend of Paul's place to practice with his band, 'cause on weekends Paul and them played at coffeehouses and clubs. And Paul kept reminding me, like I was mental, that if I was gonna sing with his band, I had to stay straight and not mess with any drugs or alcohol.

I weren't planning on messing with nothin', but I got tired of him always saying I might, like any minute I gonna get high, so I said, "You cain't be bossing me round. Without me, you ain't got a band. Mick ain't gonna do no New York City without me. Anyways, a band ain't no good without they bein' high. Ain't never heard of a one that weren't playin' high."

Paul said, with his face getting hot red, "You want to sing in the band, you stay clean, period! Don't think you can't be replaced, because you can."

I stayed clean for a while, but then three things happened kinda all at once.

First, Paul told me to keep my eyes and my hands off Jed, the drummer, 'cause he were trouble.

Well, if someone tell me don't look, all I can do is look. I never woulda even noticed Jed in the back with all his drums round him if Paul hadn't said don't, 'cause he were a white dude and I ain't usually interested in white.

Turned out Jed were a binger. He went on binges of drinkin' and druggin' and gettin' it so bad, he couldn't even perform, and they had to cancel gigs 'cause of it. That's why Lisa did drums when we recorded up at the Shoals: Jed were on a binge.

I told Paul to lose the guy if he couldn't perform. They was plenty of other drummers in the world. But Paul said Jed were his old, old friend from home, and they go way back. He said that like going way back meant something important, but way I was lookin' at it, were just a lot of bad history between them and they was both better off without each other.

Anyways, when Paul weren't looking, I were checking out Jed. The dude kinda had a big head, made me think of a horse's head 'cause of his chestnut hair and chestnut eyes and the way his teeth looked all the same size—big. He wore his hair real long and were like girl's hair, the way it shined. He looked real tall sittin' at his drums, but when he stood up he were just average, so most of his height musta been in his body. I gave the dude the sexy shoulder, and he winked back at me. That's all it were, at first, just flirting stuff.

Then come the second thing that happened. Paul got a call from Lisa, and he invited her to come stay for the weekend.

I heard what he were saying on the phone and when he hung up I said, "Where's that bitch gonna stay? Ain't no room for her here. Ain't barely room for me."

Paul weren't half paying attention to me 'cause his mind still were on his phone call. It took him a couple of seconds to hear me.

"Oh," he said. "That's no problem. The couch pulls out into a bed. You two can sleep together."

"No way! And how come I been sleeping on it like it just a couch if it be a bed, too?"

Paul flopped down in one of his chairs like he just too exhausted for words. He let his head fall back against the chair and said to me, "It's more comfortable as a couch. There's a bar that runs under the mattress that's really uncomfortable." He lifted his head. "If you want, you two can pull out the mattress and set it on the floor."

"Ain't no way I gonna sleep with her. She got bad breath and BO, too."

Paul laughed. "She does not. Okay, we'll sleep out here, and you can have my bed."

I jumped up from the keyboard, where I been sitting, and said, "I'll sleep with her, then, 'cause that girl be afraid of men."

Paul shook his head. "Liar," he said.

Third thing that happened, our song come out on the radio, so real soon we was gonna go on tour!

It happened when Lisa come to town, so she were there to celebrate, and her and Paul was acting like they drunk when they ain't had nothin' but Cokes. Everybody were acting silly, and they was laughing and cheering and listening on the radio for it to come on again. The only two people who wasn't flying round drunk-happy was me and Jed. All that day I been listening to Paul and Lisa talk, and they didn't hardly say nothin' that I could join in on, 'cause it were about college stuff and books they both read and stuff going on in the Middle East. Paul kept saying the word *resonates* to her all the time, too, which were gettin' on my one nerve, 'cause what the hell were the meaning of that word? He pulled a book off his shelf and handed it to Lisa. He said the book really resonates with him. Later, he played her a song he said really resonates, especially the chorus. Then when we was walking in this dingy city park that had more garbage than flowers, he said how he missed the mountains, and he says this long poem about the mountains to her and tells her it really resonates.

I said, "You know what, Paul, your ass really resonates," and him and Lisa looked at one another and burst out laughing, like what I said be their own private joke, and like *I* were the joke! I wanted to rip both their fool heads off for laughing at me, and I didn't say nothin' more to them till we got out of the garbage garden and Luckie from the band come up and said we was just on the radio on the classical music station that sometimes plays jazz and blues.

Then Jed were in a sulk 'cause it weren't him on the drums playing on the radio, and nobody could say yet if he was gonna go to New York City with us or not, and maybe just Lisa be the one going. So him and me didn't neither of us like Lisa, and weren't neither of us celebrating, even when the pizzas and beer and Cokes come.

We was all over at Luckie's place, which was a apartment over a bunch of offices. He called it a loft 'cause it were one big room he had to divide up with hanging sheets and tall bookcases. Well, that loft were real big, so I knew Paul wouldn't see when I gone up to Jed and asked him if he got anything stronger than Co-Cola and beer laying round we could dip into.

Jed grinned a big horse-faced grin at me when I asked him. Then he pulled on my arm, and we run outta there.

We started out at Jed's place, which weren't nothin' but a dirt pit, far as I could tell. I sat down on a brown-and-tan couch that coulda come straight outta Patsy and Pete's stink house, it smelled so bad. Jed run off to his bathroom, then come out again with a bottle in his hand. He shook it in my face, and I leaned away.

"What they be?" I asked him.

He said, "I stole these from the drugstore where I work. They're tranquilizers." He laughed and shook the bottle again.

"You want?" he asked.

I stood up, shovin' him and his stupid pills away. "I don't want no sleep medicine," I said. "I wanna get happy. Now what you got that can get me singin' and dancin' round here?"

Jed flicked the lid off the pill bottle with his thumb and popped some of them pills into his mouth. He swallowed and said, "Don't have much here, just vodka. The rest we'll have to dig up someplace else."

"Well, vodka be fine to start with," I said, "but it ain't great. Why you bring me here when you got nothin' but nothin', anyways?"

Jed winked at me, then got the vodka bottle out from under his couch, gettin' down on his belly right near my feet to do it. Didn't know what that fool were doing till he brought out the juice, so I were trying to step outta his way and fell over on top of him. He liked that real good. He rolled over and grabbed on to me and brung his legs round me so I couldn't stand back up again. We sat face to face like that and drank that juice hard and straight, and I could feel myself going soft and fuzzy inside. Jed tried to put the moves on me, seeing how I was woozy, but I weren't doin' nothin' with my clothes off in that stink hole, so we set out for a place near where me and Paul was living, and scored us some good junk.

Then we took it on over to Paul's clean white apartment, and I put on some frisky music and got dancing and glancing Jed's way. He were already too stoned to give me much notice, though. I could see sweat runnin' down his face. His face were real pale, too, and I said maybe he better lie down awhile 'cause he didn't look so good. He tore at his shirt like it chokin' him round the neck and said to never mind him, 'cause he be fine. Then he went to the bathroom, and I sat on the couch, feeling kind of funny myself. I looked up at the bookshelves and saw a sunrise on all them books of Paul's. There were such a beautiful sunrise come suddenly, with all the colors of the rainbow spreading out like fingers on all them books, I lay back and sung a song to the sunrise.

Later, when Paul and Lisa come in, I were laying on the counter between the kitchen and the living room, with my feet up in the air. Cain't remember what I said to them when I seen them, but whatever, it made Paul so mad, he pulled me off the counter hard, and I fell to the floor and my legs was bruised for weeks.

I remember Paul asked where Jed be at, though, and I said in the bathroom, but Jed weren't there after all. He were layin' in Paul's bed. He were laying in there, dead.

chapter forty-one

TOO BAD IT WEREN'T me that was dead, 'cause I were the one that got in all the trouble. Were like I be the one killed him.

The ambulance took me and Jed to the hospital, and first the doctors pumped out my stomach, which were the worst kind of torture. A lady doctor then come up to me and said that Jed got hold of some bad stuff and I were probably a very lucky young lady to still be alive. Then the police come along and want to know where we got ahold of the junk and all kinds of questions about Jed I didn't know the answers to, but they kept at me like I just be lyin' to them.

Now and then I saw Paul outside the room I got put in, but he never come in or talked to me till it were at long last time to go home.

I said I were sorry, when we was in the car going home, and that it weren't my fault, and Paul said, "Shut up!" real loud and hard, so I shut up. We got to his apartment and Lisa were there waiting for us in her pink bathrobe and slippers, like a worried little housewife.

"What happened?" she asked. "Is everything all right?"

Paul didn't want her to talk, neither, 'cause I seen how he clenched his jaw hard so the muscles showed through on his face.

He turned to me and said, "Pack your things and get out of here."

Me and Lisa spoke at the same time. Lisa said, "Paul, it's after midnight. You can't just throw her out."

I said, "Where I gonna go? I ain't got no place to go."

Paul tore at his hair, he were so angry, and I ain't never seen nobody do that before. He growled and tore at his hair. Then he turned on me and yelled in my face, "Get out! Get out! Get out!"

I got out. I didn't take nothin' with me but what I had on, but I didn't go far. I lay on the floor outside Paul's door and fell to sleep soon as my head touched the cool wood floor.

I DIDN'T WAKE till I heard Lisa say, "Thank God."

I opened my eyes and looked straight up and saw Paul and Lisa standing above me, in the doorway. I groaned. I felt all banged up everywhere on my body, including in my stomach. I sat up, and Paul backed up into the apartment a bit.

Lisa squatted down next to me. "Are you all right? Come on, let me help you up."

Didn't want Paul's little housewife helping me do nothin,' so I pulled away from her and said, "I be fine if you could stop breathin' on me."

Lisa looked up at Paul and said, "You want me to stay?"

Paul said, "No, I can handle it."

I said, "I ain't a it."

Paul said, "Get up and get inside." His voice were his hard voice, but it sounded flat and bored, too, like he really didn't care what I did.

I groaned and stood up and got inside. Him and Lisa said their sweet good-byes, whispering to each other and kissing real quick. Then Paul turned and come inside with me.

"You cannot live here with me any longer," he said. He were still in his sweatpants and undershirt, and his hair were all poky. He were scowling at me good, but with his silly hair standing up, I weren't scared.

He went to the counter to show me my stuff all packed up and waiting for me. "I put your things in here," he said, patting a backpack. "I put some money in the front zipper. You can keep the pack."

I come into the room more. "Don't need your money or that pack. I can get me a job any old day. I don't have to go on your stupid-ass New York trip to make me some money. I can take care of myself."

"That's a laugh."

"I been doing fine without you for all these years, I can do fine again. Anyways, thanks for all your music lessons. They was nice." I pulled the pack off the counter and put it on my shoulder.

Paul crossed his arms over his chest and said, "Yes, it *was* nice. Why did you have to ruin it?"

"You be the one who ruined it. You the one had Lisa come over."

Paul gave a big sigh and shook his head like he didn't know what to say.

I looked at his feet. He had long knobby toes that looked like he went all the time in too tight shoes. I shrugged and said kinda quiet, "I don't know why I always ruin things. Don't know I'm ruining something till I ruin it. I don't know why it be my fault Jed be dead. I don't know why." I looked up at Paul, and he let go his arms from his chest and let them hang loose. It made his whole body sag.

"The drugs, Leshaya, the drugs! We had an agreement, remember? I thought you liked staying here. I thought you wanted to change."

"I never agreed to nothin', and I didn't make Jed take them tranquilizers he stole. He done all that on his own. You just lookin' for someone to blame 'cause you sorry he dead."

Paul exploded when I said that. His arms was flappin', and he said, "Yeah, I am! He was my oldest friend! You killed my best friend, and you don't show an ounce of remorse!"

"I didn't kill nobody! He were *your* best friend, so why didn't you help him? Why you let him go on all his binges? Why didn't you get him to a rehab place or something if you cared so much? You was his best friend."

Paul's eyes looked wild and hot. "How was I supposed to stop him? What should I have done, tied the both of you up?"

"What were I supposed to do? How come it be my fault just 'cause I were with him? How were I supposed to know them drugstore pills don't mix good with alcohol? What if we both died? What if I took them pills, too? Then who's fault it be? Yours! We was at your place, and I were livin' with you. So goin' by the way you think, it would be your fault. It be all your fault!"

Paul held his hands up and said, "All right, let's stop this. Okay, you're right, it wasn't just your fault."

"Damn straight!"

"But the things you did, you *are* responsible for them."

I felt too tired to keep standing up, so I flopped down in one of Paul's chairs, thinking he were gonna yell at me for sitting, but he didn't. He just come over in front of me and kept talking and yelling, with his hands flinging here and there to help him make his point.

He said, "What you do doesn't just affect you! You

hurt me and the band, too. The trip to New York, re-member? Do you ever think even a minute ahead?" He picked up a pillow and threw it back down on the couch. "Man!" he said. "What you do hurts anybody else who cares about you, not just you. Don't you get that?"

"Well, that list ain't long. Got nobody caring about me, so I don't got to worry 'bout who I be hurtin'."

"*Agh!*" Paul said, or something like that. "You don't let anybody care about you. You don't let anybody get close enough!"

"Yeah, it be my fault again. Funny how it always be my fault."

Paul raised up his hand. "Whose fault is it, then, if it isn't yours? Man!" He dropped hisself down on the couch. "Man!" he said again. He had his head back and were looking up at the ceiling. Then he lifted up and sat forward, looking at me again. "You know, you act like you're the only one. Like the whole world is against *just* you. Just because your life's been tough doesn't mean you're excused from being responsible. Like it or not, you *do* live in society."

"Yeah, whatever," I said, and I shrugged 'cause I didn't know what he were meaning about that living-in-society stuff. I guess he thought when I said *whatever*, that it meant I didn't care 'bout what he said, 'cause he sprung up from the couch like I just stepped on his one last nerve. He had his fists held tight on the sides of his body, like he were trying not to beat me up, and all these veins popped out his neck.

"Get out!" he shouted, raising one of his stiff-angry arms and pointing at the door. "Go on, get your things and get out!"

I knew he weren't gonna let me back in again, so I grabbed my stuff and left.

chapter forty-two

I WALKED TO THE Krispy Kreme doughnut shop and bought me a sack of doughnuts and coffee and sat outside in the garbage park to eat them. Were a cold day for what I had on—Paul's black jeans and his white undershirt. The sky were gray, and weren't nothin' blooming in the trees, and no birds singin'. Nobody else were in the park but me. I stuffed my last bite of doughnut in my mouth and tossed my sack and coffee cup on the ground with the rest of the garbage. I took Paul's pack and the diaper bag I come to him with, and walked along the street, and the wind blew cold at me.

A old man who looked like he got one of his eyes shot out come walking toward me. I hung close to the building I were at, and he went on by, stinkin' of piss and old dead stuff. Right behind him a lady in a bright red coat come along walking fast, her high heels clicking on the sidewalk all smart and snappy sounding, like this be her special day. I wanted to follow her and see where she going so bright and fast like that, but I didn't. I kept walking the way I been walking till I come to a pay phone. I set my junk down, pulled out some quarters from my pocket, and paid the phone. I dialed Mama Linda's number—what else. I let it ring six times. I started to hang up, then I heard a voice on the line. I put the phone back to my ear.

"Hello?" I said.

"Hello?" Were a sleepy scratchy voice on the other end.

"This is—this is Jane. This be Janie. Who this?"

The voice sounded brighter. "Jane! My Jane? It's—this is your mama Linda!"

"Oh hey, Mama," I said, trying to sound like I knew she gonna be there and I didn't care much about it.

"Where are you? Are you here in Gulf Shores?"

"No, ma'am. I'm in Atlanta."

"Oh." Mama Linda said, and she sounded like she were sad, real sad.

"But I were thinkin'—I were thinkin' I could come see you. Just, you know, come see you?"

"Yeah? Well, good. Come on down. You remember where I live?"

"No, don't remember nothin' but this number. But I can take a bus, and maybe you could pick me up at the station?"

"I don't have a car anymore. You get a taxi and I'll pay

for it, okay? I'm the street just after Orange Beach Way, on the right. It's a little dead-end road. I'm the only house on it."

"Yeah, okay. Well, okay—bye."

"Yeah, bye."

I hung up the phone and stared at it. I didn't move for a long time. I couldn't move for a long, long time.

chapter forty-three

THE TAXI DRIVER passed Mama Linda's road twice before he decided the little dirt path with all the tall grass
growing along it, like nobody been on it for years, had
to be Mama Linda's street. He turned onto the dirt
and drove slow, catching the tall beach grass in his an-
tenna.

I stuck my hand out the window and let the grass hit
my hand. Weren't but a bitty road. Mama Linda's house
stood at the end. It were a wood house, beaten gray by
lots of rain and wind and sand. It stood high up on stilts
and had a long set of stairs leading up to the door.

I didn't wait for Mama Linda to pay the driver, 'cause
Paul had put me enough money in my pack to pay for
the bus and taxi rides myself. So I paid, and the taxi
backed up the street and out to the main road, 'cause
there weren't nowhere to turn round first.

I went slow up the steps of Mama Linda's house and

stopped when I got to the top. From up there I could see the Gulf and people on the beach and seagulls flying round over them. Their screeching noise set my teeth to hurting. I turned away from the water and knocked on the door 'cause weren't no doorbell, and I waited. I knocked again. I waited again. Nobody come to the door. I didn't know if Mama Linda tricked me on purpose or her mind were just too blown to tell me straight where she lived.

I looked in the window and saw a white room with beach-type furniture in it. The wood floor were painted a deep blue, and all the cloth on the chair cushions was blue and white. Everything were blue and white and yellow, bright yellow. Didn't look like a room Mama Linda would have. Were too fresh-clean and cheerful, and warm looking.

I knocked again but nobody come. I tried the door and it opened. I stepped inside and called out, "Mama Linda? It's me. It Leshaya. I mean—it Janie." I kept walking through the room calling out, moving toward the kitchen I could see at the back. "Mama Linda?" I saw a room to the right, and I looked in at it. Were a bedroom, but she weren't there. "Mama? Mama Linda, it's me, Janie."

I come to a bathroom also off on the right side, then I come to the kitchen back of the main room with still another door on the right of it, but it were closed. I knocked on it. "Hey, Mama Linda? Hello?" I opened the door slow and looked in. The room were dark 'cause all the curtains be pulled, but I could see someone were laying in the bed. "Mama Linda? It me, Janie."

A head lifted up from the pillow. "Janie? Little face? You got here so fast. I just hung up the phone with you." Her voice were sleepy-groany, like when we talked on the phone.

"No, Mama Linda, that were hours ago. It be almost five o'clock."

"Come here, let me see you. Open a curtain, will you? Let me see you."

I pulled back the curtains and saw the ocean outta every window. I went to Mama Linda's bed. She raised up her arm to touch me, and I seen all her ugly old veins.

"You sick?" I asked, even though I could see she were real sick. Weren't never more than skin and bones, anyway, but now she were hardly no skin, 'cause it were so thin-looking and had them veins popped out so ugly. She didn't much look like herself at all. She had just bits of hair and more veins on her head. Her neck looked too long, and her eyes looked deep and hollowed out. She blinked at me.

"You're still pretty," she said to me. "You look just like me."

I backed away from her bed. "No, I don't. What's wrong with you? You got some disease? You got that AIDS disease?"

Mama Linda sighed, and it sounded like it come from so deep inside her body, like it be her last breath.

I backed away some more.

"Yeah, baby, I got AIDS." She smiled and her lower lip cracked open in the middle and blood come out. She grabbed a tissue off her bedside table and wiped her lips.

"I cain't stay long," I said. "I just come to say hi, and then I gotta go, 'cause, see, I'm a singer. I got this song come out on the radio, and I gonna be goin' on tour with it."

Mama Linda nodded. "It's all right. I'm not going to be hanging around here much longer myself."

"Yeah. Shouldn't you be in a hospital or something?"

"No. I want to be here. This is my home. I've come back home. Do you remember this house? It was your grandparents' house, remember?"

"Don't remember no grandparents."

"Right, they both died before you were a year old." Mama Linda lay her head back on her pillow and closed her eyes like any minute she gonna fall back asleep—or fall off dead. "They left me the beach house, and my brother, Len, got the big house," she said. Her voice sounded tired of talking.

"You got a brother?"

"No, not really." She opened her eyes and looked round like she were hunting for something. "Now that I'm dying, he's sending me money, but last time I saw him was years and years ago. He lives in Italy." Mama Linda tried to laugh, and her lip cracked more and got to bleeding again. "Parents thought if I got the big house, I'd sell it for drugs. The place had been in the family since before the Civil War. Brother Len didn't even wait for their graves to get cold. He sold it and moved to Italy." Mama Linda sounded all out of breath. She took in a couple of deep breaths, and I watched her chest rise and fall, and rise and fall, big and bony.

"Here I am, now, and I still got the beach house," she said.

"Yeah," I said, "you still got the beach house. Sold off other things, but you still got the beach house."

Mama Linda lifted her head. She dabbed at her bloody lip with her tissue. "I fixed it up myself," she said, like she didn't get my meaning. "I was always good at making a place look nice. Look around, you'll see. I could have been an interior decorator." She looked at her tissue, then looked at me. "Could you pour me some water? Here, on the table."

I looked at her bedside table with the phone and the tissues and the pitcher of water and the glass. There was bottles and bottles of pills there, too, and I didn't want to touch nothin' of it. Her AIDS germs was all over the place. She were bleeding right there in front of me. I turned and run. I run out her room and straight out the house.

chapter forty-four

I HURRIED DOWN the stairs so fast, my diaper bag come off my shoulder and fell down in front of me, rolling down the steps. I were kinda leaning forward, reaching for it and chasing after it, so I didn't see the old lady standing at the bottom till I almost crashed into her. She had a bag of groceries in her hands. I stopped short and said, "Oh!"

The lady smiled. She had a big nose. She said, "You're Janie, right? I'm Mrs. Trane. Your mother said you were coming. Sorry I wasn't here when you arrived. Would you take this for me?" She handed me the bag. "I've got another one in the car."

I stood with the bag in my hand and watched her limp to her car, like she got one leg way shorter than the other one.

The lady limped back toward me with her second bag of groceries and nodded for me to go on up the steps. "I'll follow," she said.

"Oh. Well, okay, I'll take this bag up, but I ain't stayin,' 'cause I got to be goin'."

I climbed back up the stairs, and she come after me with her bag, making heavy clomping noises on the steps, so they creaked and groaned like they gonna bust apart. I went back to the kitchen and set the groceries on the counter.

Mama Linda called out, "Melissa? Janie came. I think I scared her off."

Mrs. Trane set her bag down and went to the doorway of Mama Linda's room. "Nonsense," she said. "Your Janie's right here." She turned to me and made a motion for me to come to her. I come to the door but I didn't look in. I looked at my shoes, old plastic things I stole from a Kmart.

"See, here she is." Then she said to me, "Your mama's so glad you've come. It's right for the two of you to patch things up now."

I looked up. I saw Mama Linda sitting up in her bed. The pitcher of water were on the floor and so were the water. Her glass lay tipped over in her lap.

The old lady limped into the room and picked up the pitcher. It were just a plastic thing, so it didn't break. "Janie, get me a sponge off the sink," the lady said to me. "Let's clean this mess up for your mama."

I did it. I got her the sponge. I come into the room and handed it to Mrs. Trane. She didn't take it. She nodded and said, "Yes, that's the one to use, good for you. Don't miss the bit under the bed. I'll go get dinner started." She headed out the room. "Linda, I hope you've got a big appetite tonight. I'm making lasagna."

I got on the floor to clean up the water. I looked up at Mama Linda. Didn't think she ever in her life had a big appetite, but I knew I were hungry. I hadn't had nothin' since the sack of doughnuts I ate that morning.

Mama Linda talked to me while I were sponging up her floor. "I didn't mean to scare you before, little face."

"Didn't scare me. I got places to go."

"I don't think so."

I stood up and squeezed the sponge into the pitcher. "I told you I be a singer now. You don't believe me, turn on your radio." I got back on the floor and wiped up under the bed, holding my breath the whole time, case they be germs so close to the bed.

"What I don't believe is if you had anywhere else to go, you'd be here."

"Well, I ain't stayin'. I were just curious about you. I'll be leavin' after dinner."

Mama Linda slumped down in the bed. "I need to rest," she said, like what I just said sucked all her energy out.

"Yeah, okay." I got up and grabbed the pitcher without thinking. I were halfway out the door when I realized I were holding something her AIDS-germy hands had touched. I dropped the pitcher on the floor.

Mrs. Trane come from the kitchen to see what the noise be.

I looked at her. "I touched the pitcher. Didn't mean to touch the pitcher."

"It's all right. You won't get AIDS touching your mama's things. I'll clean this up and you go wash your hands. I left a head of lettuce in a bowl. You can tear the lettuce for us."

I hurried off to get my hands washed. I run them under the hottest water I could get and squirted dishwashing liquid all over them. The soap made so much suds, I couldn't get it to go down the drain.

Mrs. Trane come in with the pitcher and seen what I done. "Not much experience in a kitchen, have you? Well, now you know a little dishwashing liquid goes a long way." She set the pitcher on the counter and waved her hands round in the sink, keeping the water running. Bit by bit the soap go down. She handed me a towel to dry my hands, then showed me how I were supposed to tear the lettuce.

"Yeah," I said. "I seen that done before."

"Good, I'll leave you to it, and I'll work on the lasagna. We'll be a team, okay? We'll make your mother a nice hot dinner."

I said, "I don't know why. She ain't gonna eat none of it. Don't look like she ate nothin' for years."

"Do you think we should just let her starve to death?" The old lady were cutting up a onion, and it were stinging my eyes.

I blinked and blinked and kept tearing at the lettuce.

"She's starving her own self. Why not give her a bowl of cereal, or something? It be easier, and most likely all the same to her. Won't eat that, neither."

"If you were dying, is that the way you would want to be treated? Your mother's still alive. She deserves some dignity and respect, don't you think?"

"I think she got what she deserved," I said. "She got AIDS."

chapter forty-five

TURNED OUT THE OLD LADY could cook. Were a long, long time since I had a meal so good. We had our dinner on trays that sat on stands, and ate in Mama Linda's room. Mrs. Trane opened some of the windows, and a bit of breeze was coming through. She held a fork-ful of lasagna up for Mama Linda to eat, but like I said would happen, she didn't want none.

Mrs. Trane said, "You have to try the salad. Your baby made this salad all by herself. Look how pretty she cut up the tomatoes." She lifted a forkful of salad to Mama's mouth and Mama Linda took it. She chewed on it a long time, staring at me all the while she doing it.

I looked down and scooped up more lasagna. I were already on my second helping, and Mrs. Trane and Mama Linda had hardly got anywhere with their first.

I heard Mama Linda swallow, 'cause it were so loud. Then she said to Mrs. Trane, "Janie looks just like me."

"No, I don't," I said. "Woman, you need to look in a mirror."

Mama Linda smiled at me and licked her dry lips. "I think I am looking in a mirror."

I stood up and took up my plate of food. "I'm gonna eat in the other room."

I ate at the table in the main room and looked out at the water view. All that water didn't look so scary through a plate of glass. When I finished I got up and went to the bathroom, then lay down on the couch, only weren't a couch, really. Mrs. Trane said all the furniture be made of wicker, which were like thin painted-white strips of wood wound this way and that. When you sat in a chair, it made creaking noises like it were giving way. The couchlike one had a long cushion on it and all these pillows for the back. I took a pillow for my head and lay down 'cause I be so tired. Later Mrs. Trane come in and waked me and said I could sleep in the other bedroom, 'cause she had her own home to go to.

I got up and dragged to the bedroom and got in the bed and fell back asleep real fast. Don't know how long I slept when Mama waked me up calling from her bed. I climbed out my bed and shuffled myself to her room. The full moon were out over the water making it light in there.

"I need help going to the bathroom," Mama Linda said to me when I got to her doorway.

"Okay," I said. "Where be the old lady? I'll tell her."

"She's gone home. Just help me up and let me hold on to you."

"You gonna touch me? No way, I don't think so."

I turned round and went back to my bed and crawled in. Mama Linda called for me. I put the pillow over my head. She kept calling. Seemed like half the night she were calling. I didn't do nothin' 'bout it, and finally, she stopped.

Next morning the old lady come wake me up and tell me to go to Mama Linda's room 'cause I got to help clean up.

I pulled on Paul's pants from the day before. They was on the floor by my bed, where I didn't remember putting them, 'cause I didn't never remember taking them off. I slipped on my shoes and followed Mrs. Trane to Mama Linda's bedroom.

"If I gotta sponge up water again, I want to wear a pair of them rubber gloves I seen you wear last night."

"You can sure wear the latex gloves if you want, but it isn't water you'll be cleaning. It's pee."

I stopped walking. "I ain't cleaning up no Mama Linda pee. She make a mess, let her clean it up."

Mrs. Trane grabbed my arm, and for a old lady she were way strong. It surprised me.

"Hey, lady, let go a me!"

I tried twisting out from her, but she got a death grip on me I couldn't shake off.

"You go clean up the mess, and maybe tonight you'll

think twice about leaving your mother to pee in her bed."

"She ain't my responsibility. Now let go, I'm gettin' outta here."

The old lady twisted my arm! She twisted my arm like she gonna break it off. "You're going to go in and clean up your mother's mess."

"You gonna break my arm if I don't?"

The old lady pulled on me, dragging me to Mama's bedroom. She shoved me into the room, and before I could turn round to fight back, she done closed the door and locked it with a key.

I stood facing the door, breathing hard. I cussed her out good and kicked the door, but weren't no sound coming from the other side.

"She thinks we're going to patch things up," Mama Linda said behind me.

I whipped myself around. "I ain't doin' nothin' with you!"

Mama Linda was sitting hunched in a chair, wrapped in a blanket and shivering. There were bits of egg spilt on the blanket. She looked at me with her hollowed-out eyes and nodded. "I know. I know what I've done to you."

"Yeah, so do I. You give me away. You traded me off for heroin like I some kinda nothin'! Well, you nothin' to me!"

I marched over to her set of windows facing out at the water. Each window had a crank to open them up. I took one and turned it.

"I ain't stayin' round with you," I said. The window opened and a big wind blowed in the room. I put my head to the screen and looked down. Were a long way down. I wouldn't get far on broken legs. I cranked the window shut and turned round.

"You clean?" Mama Linda asked me.

"What?" I said, like she some pesky fly I want to smash.

"You take drugs?"

"No! I ain't stupid like you. I got me a life. I got talent. Don't need no drugs."

I marched across the room and pounded on the door. "Let me out! I gotta pee!"

Mama Linda said, "Why don't you use my bed. It worked for me." She laughed a croaky stale laugh like it been sitting inside her chest a long time, then took a deep sucking breath.

I pounded on the door again.

"Sing to me," Mama Linda said behind me, sucking another breath.

I turned round. "Never. Ain't never gonna sing for you. You ain't never gonna hear me sing nothin', so shut up."

Mama Linda lifted her blanket closer round her face. Her lips and eyelids looked blue. She said, "It's just if you really can sing, then I could probably tell you who your father is, that's all. Then I would know."

I pointed at her. "You lie! You ain't gonna tell me. You don't have no idea who he be. I know all about it, 'cause

I got my own—" I shut my mouth and didn't say no more.

"Your own what? You don't know anything about my life."

"Ain't my fault."

"Didn't say it was." She took another long suck of air.

I kicked back on the door and yelled out. "She gettin' sick sittin' in this chair. She breathin' like she gonna die in here. You better come see."

I didn't get no answer. I shouted, "You out there? Hey! You out there?"

No answer.

I looked at Mama Linda sunk in her blanket. She were lookin' scary like she really gonna die on me. I big-time wanted outta there. I didn't want the blame for her dyin', too.

"Okay," I said. "Okay, I gonna sing for you. I got just the song, 'cause I wrote it myself, and if you want proof, I got it written down in music with my name on it. See, 'cause I learned something. I can read music and write it down and everything. I can play a song on the piano. You didn't know that, huh?"

I went to the bed and stuck on a pair of them latex gloves sitting in a box on the table. I pulled off the blankets and sheets and got the wet cloth I seen sitting in a bowl of soap water. I wrung it out and wiped down the plastic mattress cover. I cleaned it off and sung my song. I sung about listening in the dark for footsteps that never come. Half the way through, I stopped with the cleaning and looked out at a boat sailing on the water. I kept singing. I sung to the boat and to the water and the seagulls, and I sung to Mama Linda sittin' shivering and sucking up air behind me. I sung out my pain and Mama Linda heard that. She heard exactly what been hidin' dark in my soul for all my life. I know 'cause when I turned round, she were crying tears on her blanket.

chapter forty-six

WHEN I FINISHED singing, I went back to cleaning up pee, and Mama Linda sat sniffling and sucking up air and snot. We didn't neither of us say nothin', but didn't matter, 'cause I felt like my song said all I ever needed to say to Mama Linda. I felt like something got washed clean and clear inside of me.

I took the clean stack of sheets from off the chair I were sitting eating dinner in the night before, and made up Mama Linda's bed. I saw a blanket folded on top of a tall white chest I had to stand on tiptoe to reach, and I put that on before I added back the cover and the other blankets. Then I went to Mama Linda, who were still crying and wiping her snot on her blanket. I told her to let go the blanket, and I pulled at her arms to get her standing. She were so light were like her bones got all hollowed out. I saw old marks on the inside of her arms. Old tracks from her heroin days.

I said, "Now you be on other drugs, huh? Now you be legal with them bottles you got by the bed?"

Mama Linda didn't say nothin'. It took all her wobbling strength to make it to the bed and sit down on it. I picked up her legs and her feet, which looked so big and knobby dangling off them bone legs of hers, and I careful put them under the covers. I pulled up the blanket and covered her up good. Mama Linda slunk down, sighed deep, and closed her eyes. I turned to leave, and her hand come up on my arm. I looked back at her.

She opened up her eyes and said, "I'm pretty sure your father was a man named English. Howard Lee English. He died. Overdose. Long time ago."

I handed Mama a tissue off her table, and she wiped her nose.

"Were he black or white?" I asked.

Mama Linda raised her brows. "White. I never slept with a black man."

"Oh," I said. I left her side and grabbed up the wet sheets.

"He had a beautiful voice. A rich, butterfat tenor." Mama sucked in her breath with every sentence she talked to me. "He wanted to sing and compose"—big breath—"music, but his father wanted him in banking"—big breath—"Howard went to Wharton"—big breath—"but got kicked out second semester. He died"—big breath—"New Year's Eve. I think he OD'd on purpose. All he wanted to do was"—big breath—"sing."

I were standing by the door, keeping the wet sheets away from my body. The smell were sharp in my nose.

"My name be Jane English, then?"

Mama closed her eyes. She sighed another deep sigh, and I watched her chest lift up and sink down.

I turned and knocked on the door real soft. I heard Mrs. Trane limp toward the door. She unlocked it and stepped back.

I come through the door. "Mama Linda's sleepin', I think," I said.

Mrs. Trane peeked in over my shoulder. She nodded at me. "Good. You did a good job. You can set the sheets in the washing machine. It's in that closet in the kitchen there. Then why don't you take a shower, and I'll make you a pancake breakfast."

I did what she said to do, then took me a shower. The water run down hot on my body and it felt good. I soaped myself up and rinsed myself clean. Ain't never felt so clean.

chapter forty-seven

I LIVED WITH MAMA LINDA till she died. I lived with her almost three and a half months. Took her that long to die, even though every day I were there looked like it gonna be her last one.

We didn't never talk again 'bout my daddy or 'bout her life. We didn't never say nothin' 'bout my drownin' or her kidnapping me or any of that stuff, 'cause Mama had pneumonia and got put on oxygen soon after I come. Then she went into a coma and stayed like that till she died. But I told her 'bout my baby girl, Etta Harmony James, and I sung her more songs. And when my song come on the radio, which happened four times, I turned it up for her to hear and said that it be me singin'. And she heard when the radio dude asked where did this Leshaya come from, and when he said he predicted I gonna be hot, hot, hot!

I sat by Mama's bed and talked to Mama lots, and Mrs. Trane said that Mama could hear me even if she be in a coma. So I told her how I were lyin' when I said I didn't take no drugs, but I said I were gonna try not to get into them no more. And I told her 'bout Paul and Harmon, who been nice to me, and how I caused them no end of trouble. I told her all 'bout that. Then I said that I bet she made up that story 'bout my daddy and his singing and him being white and named English. I told her how his name sounded made up. I said I bet she didn't even know who my real daddy be but that it didn't matter 'cause I understood how it could happen. And I told her how I couldn't be no Jane English 'cause I be Leshaya and I be half African American and I be a great singer and that were all I knew how to be. Mama Linda just lay there letting me say all them things to her and were like more of my soul were getting washed clean.

We gave Mama Linda warm sponge baths and changed her sheets by both of us rolling her one way and holding on while we pulled off the sheets partway, then rolling her the other way and getting all the sheets off. We didn't need to feed her nothin' 'cause she got feeding tubes and a bag that held her pee, and we just had to keep them working right and change them every once in a while.

I sat by her bed and watched her die. People always saying you can't be a little bit pregnant and you can't be a little bit dead. You either dead or you ain't, but that ain't true. Mama got a little bit more dead every day.

Every day her color got grayer, and every day she felt colder to touch, and every day she got stiller and stiller inside herself.

I asked Mrs. Trane why Mama don't die already. "What keepin' her hangin' on?"

Mrs. Trane said, "It's the survival instinct. She'll fight with every ounce in her to stay alive. Your mama always was a fighter, I'll give her that."

I watched her fight off dying. Were a quiet fight.

Watching and caring for Mama weren't all I done, 'cause the days there was long. Sometimes I went outside and walked round, but I didn't go near the water. I walked up the street the other way, where I come to all these shops full of plastic toys and T-shirts and flip-flops. I didn't never buy nothin', 'cause didn't have the money. I just turned round and come back to the house.

Most what I did when I had the time were my music. I found Paul give me two music books. They was in the pack I brung with me. I studied them both through twice.

Mrs. Trane made me what she called a silent piano by drawing the piano keys on some cardboard she had laying round her house. She said I could practice on the silent piano till I got to a real one again. She even brung me some piano books she had from when she used to play years and years ago.

I practiced some, but weren't as fun without the music.

Me and Mrs. Trane talked together lots, too. We talked while we worked round Mama, and we talked while we made our meals, and sometimes we just sat and talked.

I asked Mrs. Trane how long she knew Mama Linda, and she said off and on all Mama's life. She said she even knew me when I were a baby girl. She said she were friends with my grandparents. I asked if she knew where I could see pictures of them and me when I were a baby.

Mrs. Trane pulled out a drawer of pictures and I saw lots, but weren't none of me. I saw ones of Mama Linda and I thought some of them be me. I saw my grandparents and they looked happy all the time. I saw Mama Linda's brother and he didn't never look happy. There was pictures of birthdays and Christmas and Halloween and going to the beach and building sandcastles and hunting for Easter eggs and when Mama Linda won a first place science prize—she got lots of pictures of that. There was pictures of Mama and Brother Len on horses and peeking out from a tent and waving from up in a tree house and sitting at a restaurant in Italy, everybody with drinks in their hands, and Mama Linda standing tilted in front of a place called the Leaning Tower of Pisa. There was all these family pictures up till Mama got to be just 'bout my age, sixteen. Then pictures of her stopped.

Mrs. Trane said how Mama got into drugs round age

fifteen. She said were a tragic story 'cause Mama were a real sweetheart before then.

She sat with me on the wicker couch with all these pictures we was passing between us and told me what she knew 'bout Mama. Weren't much.

She said, "She used to be a cheerful child. She had a real good sense of humor. Always the first to laugh at herself. Not many people are willing to laugh at themselves the way she would. And she loved children. She used to be every parent's pick as baby-sitter. But she was best at science. We all thought she'd go into science, maybe be a biologist. When she was just eleven years old she created an environmental cleanup program, and that was long before that kind of thing was popular. She used to put up signs on telephone poles, inviting people to help clean up streets and streams and ponds, and she offered free coffee and doughnuts to anyone who showed up. Paid for it with her baby-sitting money. Then, I don't know what happened. She just changed, and all her baby-sitting money went to paying for her drug habit. Then that money wasn't enough and she was robbing stores and snatching purses. Nobody knew how it happened. Nobody knew what happened."

Mrs. Trane passed me the last picture of Mama. She were standing on the beach holding up a dead stingray in her hand and smiling into the camera.

I said, "Guess we ain't never gonna find out what happened."

Mrs. Trane looked at me, and it were like she be angry with me all the sudden, and I set the pictures down and stood up, thinking I might need to run.

She pointed her finger at me and said, "You've got a little girl. You tell her. You tell her about your life. And you be honest with her. Don't let her make the same mistakes. Break the pattern, Leshaya. Change her destiny. She doesn't have to grow up just like you. I heard all you said to your mama. You and she are just alike."

"No, we ain't!" I backed away from her. "I ain't nothin' like Mama Linda."

Mrs. Trane shook her head. "Maybe you never meant to be, but you are. You've followed in her footsteps all along. You're both bridge burners."

I said, "No, I ain't. What that mean? I ain't never burnt no bridges."

Mrs. Trane looked up at me so serious and mad, her tiny eyes blinking at me. She said, "What happens when you cross over a bridge, then you turn around and burn it? Can you get back over the water?"

"No, not on that bridge you cain't."

"That Paul person you told your mama about. You had a good thing working with him. Then you burned your bridge by going against your agreement, taking those drugs, getting involved with his best friend. You see? You made it just about impossible to return. You make it impossible for anybody to have a relationship with you. You use people up. And that poor Harmon boy." Mrs. Trane shook her head and clicked her tongue.

I shrugged 'cause I didn't know what to say. Then a sound come from Mama Linda's room like Mama suddenly come awake from her coma. We both of us hurried to the room, but it weren't the sound of Mama Linda waking up, were the sound of her last dying.

chapter forty-eight

WHEN MAMA LINDA DIED, Mrs. Trane took all the hoses and stuff out her body and out her mouth. All the machines stopped making their noises.

I looked down at Mama Linda laying flat on her pillow, and she looked real peaceful. Never seen her look that way before. Looked like dying be just the right thing for her.

The medical people who brung all the equipment to the house come and took it all away again, and more medical people come and took away Mama.

We didn't have no funeral. Weren't nobody left to come to it, anyway, 'cause like Mrs. Trane said to me, Mama Linda used people up and burnt all her bridges.

Mama Linda got cremated and I got the ashes in a urn. Didn't know what I were gonna do with them. Seemed a pain to haul them round with me all the time.

Mrs. Trane said I could sprinkle them somewhere or I could leave them in the urn at the beach house, 'cause the beach house were left for me to have. Weren't no money 'cause Mama Linda spent everything, and the beach house couldn't be mine for real till I turned twenty-one. Mama Linda wrote out a legal will, and Mrs. Trane and some lawyer was in charge of it together.

Mrs. Trane said I could come live with her. She said she could help me. She told me about a fine arts school in Birmingham that were free to go to, where I could study music. She said if I didn't want that, I could take a test and get a diploma and go to a community college.

I didn't say nothin', but I already knew 'bout music. I could sing. Didn't need no college or school to sing. I were on the radio! Anyway, I couldn't be goin' to no school, 'cause it were time for me to go get my sweet Etta back. I loved my baby, and I knew if you love a baby, you s'posed to keep it and take good care of it, not give it away so it be adoped and lost, the way I been. I come to understand that, spending all my time with Mama Linda. I seen how losing Mama meant losing my own self, too, and finding her, learning something 'bout her, that give me a little bit of myself back. A mama s'posed to take care of her baby. So I made my own plans, kept secret from Mrs. Trane. I were gonna go get my baby back, then go find Mick Werner, the producer, and make my own CD with my own made-up songs.

I went home with Mrs. Trane to her house after we picked up Mama's urn, and she fixed me a dinner while I played her piano. She had a real piano in her house, and she didn't never tell me. I could really play songs I couldn't play before, 'cause I practiced on the cardboard, but Lord, it were so much better hearing the music. I played till it were time to eat, then I played till Mrs. Trane gone off to bed.

When I were sure she be asleep, I went to her purse she kept hanging on a doorknob in the kitchen and took out all her money. The lady were rich. She had a hundred and fifty dollars in her purse. I put it back on the doorknob and went to bed. I didn't sleep 'cause I wanted to be awake and gone before Mrs. Trane waked up.

Round five in the morning I called a taxi to come out to the house. I waited outside for it. When it come I climbed in and told the driver to take me to the bus station. I closed the door and looked up at the house.

Mrs. Trane were standing at her bedroom window looking down at us. The taxi pulled away and Mrs. Trane waved.

I didn't wave back. I just stared at her till I couldn't see her no more.

chapter forty-nine

I BOUGHT ME a bus ticket to Tuscaloosa. I were gonna go get my baby back. My Etta Harmony James. I were gonna take her. Weren't like I be kidnapping her, though, 'cause I weren't gonna give her to nobody else. I were gonna keep her, and she already be mine. I give birth to her. I be her mama, and someday she gonna hear 'bout all my mistakes like Mrs. Trane told me to do so she don't do them, too.

I got on the bus and sat down next to a white dude who kept wanting to talk to me. He said I be real pretty. He touched my hair, but I didn't pay him no mind. All I wanted to do were get my baby back and get singin' again.

Were dark by the time I got to the Jameses' house. I felt shaky walkin' up the long driveway, and kinda sick to my stomach 'cause I were nervous 'bout how I gonna get my baby. The house looked extra giant in the dark.

I went up to a kitchen window and looked in, and

there be Mr. James cookin' at the stove, and there be a little girl standing on a step stool and shoving paper plates on the table. I wondered who that be and thought at first Mr. James and Mrs. James adopted themselves another little child.

Then I knew. It just come to me, *bam!* My baby, Etta, don't be no little baby no more. She be more 'n two years old. That girl going round the table be mine, she be my Etta Harmony James. I felt all swolled with pride and had to step back a bit from the window to think 'bout it. I forgot how she were gonna grow up while I been away. She were walking already. She like a real, whole person already. I peered back in at her, and I seen her skin had got darker and her hair were brown and had curls in it. She had fat little legs and arms and fat cheeks, and I felt so proud in my heart to see her. My Etta Harmony be so pretty and smart, the way she could do them plates at the table. She were perfect. She were the perfect little girl.

Then Harmon come into the kitchen. He didn't look no different. Same old Harmon. He picked up Etta and lifted her high. I could hear her squeal clear through the window, and my heart got all excited. She were gonna be a singer like me.

Harmon put her down, and in come a grown girl I ain't never seen before. She went round the table, fixing the paper plates so they be in place, then went to a drawer and pulled out some forks. I figured she were the new maid. She give Etta a fork to put on the table, and

Harmon come up behind her and rubbed at her back. She give him a quick kiss on the mouth. Weren't no maid.

Mr. James dumped a load of spaghetti into a bowl and set it on the table. Harmon poured out the sauce in another bowl, and he put that on the table, too. The girlfriend finished setting the table, and Harmon leaned over to say something to Etta, putting his arm round her to do it. Etta run out the room, and I heard her squeal again. Then back she come, and so did Mrs. James and their other little boy, Samson, looking taller and thin. All them sat at the table, and Etta had her a special seat set in her chair just so she could sit high like everybody else.

I didn't think how she gonna need one of them. Maybe when I took Etta back I could grab up that seat thing, too, and maybe some clothes; she gonna need clothes, and that step stool so she could set me a table the way she done them.

They got to eating, and I saw Harmon rock back in his chair and reach out his arms and put one round the back of the girlfriend's chair and one round Etta's.

I pulled away from the window. I didn't want to watch them people no more. I stood out on the lawn, not knowing how I were gonna get Etta away from them. Seemed like they hung awfully close to her. Then that picture I saw of Mama Linda and her family sitting round a table at a restaurant in Italy come to mind. They looked like a nice family in that picture. My Etta, she be in a nice family, too. She got her a good daddy and a grandmama and a grandaddy and Samson—all them folks lovin' her. And she got a special seat for her chair and pretty clothes on and a big house to live in. She got all that.

I looked at the kitchen window, at the bright light shining from it. What if I didn't take her? What if I left her? But if you love your baby you s'posed to keep her and take care of her. I stepped up to the window again, and there Etta be with a doll, feedin' it spaghetti. She were takin' good care of her baby just like I s'posed to do so she don't grow up lost.

I stepped back and turned round so I don't be seeing that cheery lighted window no more. I needed to think. What be the right thing to do? Mrs. Trane said how I got to break the pattern so Etta don't grow up like me and Mama. How I gonna do that if I don't take her? But she be so perfect. She be exactly what I always wanted to be. She got black skin. She got real African American blood running through her. She be African American—I took in a deep breath that seemed to draw on my heart and squeeze it—and all I be is a wigga.

I felt tears on my face but I brushed them away and shook my head. It time to face the truth of that. Alls I be is a wigga. I got no black in me 'cept what I put there my own self. Etta, she got it all. She got just what I always wanted—black skin and a black family to love her. Only way she gonna feel lost in her life be if I take her. Don't matter if I love her and a mama s'posed to have her. It ain't right. It don't feel right. Leaving her be loving her the right way. I know it. I feel it in my heart. I done the right and loving thing the first time, leaving her with Harmon.

I lifted my head, looked at the dark sky. And maybe it be the only right thing I ever do in my whole life, but that be okay, 'cause I think it be the one thing that matters most—that and singin'.

I brushed off the tears that kept wantin' to pour out, even when my mind told them not to. Weren't gonna cry. This be right. I gotta leave Etta and go my own way. Maybe someday I'll write her, tell her my life story. Maybe she'll hear 'bout me in the news, how I be a famous singer.

I looked cross the yard to the house next door. It looked far away through all them high bushes the Jameses had. I headed out cross the lawn toward that house, hoping the people there would let me call a taxi. Then I stopped, thought a second, and turned round and went back—right up to the Jameses' front door.

I touched the door handle. Then I reached into my pack and pulled out a cloth sack. Inside were Harmon's silver stopwatch, the only thing I stole that I didn't never lose. I stared at it a long time, thinking how I should tie the sack to the door handle and go on.

Were too much to give up that night, though. Harmon had Etta. He got the better deal. I stuffed the watch back in my pack and set out cross the lawn.